ゾンビ
ビジネス
英会話

屍速英語

活用30個學過的基本動詞，
職場英語嚇嚇叫！

KAWASEMI Co., Ltd.、交學社 著
許郁文 譯

CONTENTS

CONTENTS

登場人物介紹

Samantha

莎曼珊【人類】
湯姆的老婆。完全沒發現湯姆已經變成殭屍了。

老闆【稻草人】
湯姆所屬部門的部長。想方設法逼湯姆辭職，卻無法如願。

Boss

Medusa

梅杜莎【老闆眼線】
湯姆公司裡的時尚指標。光是盯著別人，就能讓對方石化。

Tom

湯姆【殭屍】
上班族殭屍。拚了命（？）地在上班時間偷懶。成為殭屍約一年餘。

Yasu

雅思【人類】
湯姆公司的新進工程師。女朋友是虛擬偶像。

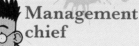

Management chief

課長【殭屍】
湯姆的課長。剛成為殭屍，尚未能從震驚中平復。

肯先生【應該是人】
湯姆的客戶。愛慕湯姆的同事費歐娜。

Mr. Ken

Sam

山姆【殭屍】
善於經營料理教室與電影院的多棲藝人。對莎曼珊情有獨鍾。

羅伯特
【貪吃鬼殭屍】

傑克
【菜鳥殭屍】

大衛
【客戶那邊的帥哥殭屍】

丹尼爾
【湯姆的殭屍朋友】

Mana

瑪娜【人類】
健身房教練。每天利用殭屍進行訓練。

殭屍研究員
【人類（醫師）】

阿玉小姐
【湯姆的鄰居】

秋霞小姐
【湯姆的鄰居】

金彬
【路人甲】

Saya   J

莎耶【人類】
湯姆公司的後輩。工作能力很強，很習慣與殭屍相處。

J【英雄】
不到緊急關頭，絕不出手相助是其座右銘。雖然常常來不及出手拯救，卻也從不反省自己。

Chandler

錢德【殭屍】
雖然討厭殭屍，但變成殭屍後，也很能適應殭屍身分。

007

本書的使用方法

　　本書的舞台設定為一個殭屍與人類和平共處的世界「英師路」。基本上，殭屍通常都是沒什麼「幹勁」的，所以書中自然也不會有什麼「艱澀的會話」了，而且日常生活中的會話大多也只用到小學或國中學過的基本動詞而已。也因此，故事主角的上班族殭屍湯姆就算廢得讓人又愛又氣（？），但大家還是可以從他的日常生活中學習到動詞的使用方法喔！

基本動詞就是有很多種解釋的動詞，本書中只會挑出一些口語常用的意思來介紹。

首先，這一頁要來教教大家掌握動詞的語感。每一個動詞都會重複出現，所以就算是沒心學英語的你，也一定能輕輕鬆鬆就了解動詞的意思。

Basic Verb 1

Have

殭屍湯姆的早餐

have-had-had/has/having

①「持有」，②「吃」，③「生病」，④「親覺」，
⑤「使～做某事，請～做某事」（使役動詞），
⑥「have to+原形動詞」（非得做某事）

Did you already have your breakfast?

你已經吃早餐了嗎？

You're still eating!
（這還在吃東西啊！）

Not yet. I have no idea what to do.

還沒啦，我完全不知道該吃什麼好啊。

⇒ have no idea
完全不知道、
沒頭緒的意思

Basic Verb 1　Have

I don't have much of an appetite today. I think I'll stop eating here.

今天沒有食欲，我差不多吃到這裡就好。

You have to go to work today.

今天不能不去公司喔！

Maybe I'll have some beer.
（也許我會喝點啤酒吧。）

Do you have any ideas about that?

那件事你有什麼想法嗎？

⇒ have an idea
有「想法」

I don't want to go to my company.
（我實在不想去公司啊。）

Column 當成「讓（別人）做某事」的意思使用時，要記得將目的語後面的動詞改回原形，（make與let在這部分的用法也一樣）。have有「讓地位較低的人做某事」的意思，有時候也會以「讓別人幫忙做某事」的意思使用。
I want to have you cut my hair.「我想請你幫我剪頭髮」。
I'll have John help with your job.「我打算讓約翰幫忙你的工作」。

010　　　　　　　　011

不用擔心艱澀難懂學不來，示範的句子都是一般生活常用的簡單句型，請務必出聲練習看看喔。

在解說該動詞稍微難懂的地方時，會再介紹一些很適合在職場上使用的例句喔。

利用會話的方式介紹慣用句，讓讀者掌握基本動詞的使用方法。無論如何，都要把這一頁讀得滾瓜爛熟喔。

透過漫畫的方式介紹實用的會話，不過有些台詞可能會惹怒對方。如果你覺得可以把責任全推給殭屍的話，那用看看也無妨。

這個專欄的動詞都是「排行榜前 10 名的基本動詞」，沒有不記住的道理。如果連背前 30 名的動詞都嫌麻煩，至少要記住專欄裡的這些動詞。這裡也會順便為大家解說動詞的核心意義。

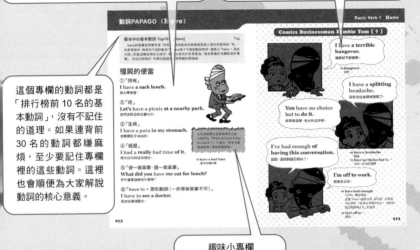

趣味小專欄

常用的慣用句會寫成例句。請想像自己身處上班族殭屍的世界，反覆地閱讀這些例句吧。如果能跟朋友一起扮演這些角色，肯定能學好英語喔。

使用這些台詞會讓你看起來英語很厲害。這些可都是能唬住別人的精選例句啲。

Have

殭屍湯姆的早餐

have-had-had/has/having

① 「持有」　② 「吃」　③ 「生病」　④ 「經歷」
⑤ 「使～做某事、請～做某事」（使役動詞）
⑥ 「have to +原形動詞（非得做某事不可）」

Did you already have your breakfast?

你已經吃早餐了嗎?

You're still eating!
你這傢伙還在吃啊!

Not yet. I have no idea what to do.

還沒啦。我完全不知道
該吃什麼好啊。

⇒ have no idea
完全不知道、
沒頭緒的意思

莎曼珊

湯姆

I don't have much of an appetite today. I think I'll stop eating here.

今天沒有食欲，我差不多吃到這裡就好。

Maybe I'll have some beer.
乾脆喝點啤酒好了。

You have to go to work today.

今天不能不去公司喔。

Do you have any ideas about that?

那件事你有什麼想法嗎？

⇒ have an idea
有「想法」

I don't want to go to my company.
我實在不想去公司。

Column 當成「讓（別人）做某事」的意思使用時，要記得將目的語後面的動詞改回原形。（make與let在這部分的用法也一樣）。have有「**讓地位較低的人做某事**」的意思，有時候也會以「**請別人幫忙做某事**」的意思使用。

I want to have you cut my hair. 「我想請你幫我剪頭髮。」
I'll have John help with your job. 「我打算請約翰協助你的工作。」

基本中的基本動詞 Top10　[Have]　　　¹⁄₁₀

　　have的首要意思雖然是「持有」，卻是能用來表現東西或人物存在與否的「有」，也是英語中，再基本不過的動詞了。have除了可當成動詞使用，還能以「have + 過去分詞」的語法構成現在完成式。現在完成式的意思是指「過去與現在有關的某件事情」。完成式用得好，代表你能說出更高等級的英語喲。

殭屍的便當

①「持有」

I have a sack lunch.

我有帶便當。

②「吃」

Let's have a picnic at a nearby park.

我們去附近的公園吃吧。

③「生病」

I have a pain in my stomach.

我覺得肚子痛痛的。

> 在吃殭屍朋友拿來的便當之前，不妨問句「What did you bring for lunch？」只是這一問有可能會讓整個午餐時間報銷喔。

④「經歷」

I had a really bad time of it.

我有段時間過得很慘。

⇒ **have a bad time**
遇到很糟的事

⑤「使～做某事、請～做某事」(使役動詞)

What did you have me eat for lunch?

你午餐要讓我吃什麼啊？

⑥「have to + 原形動詞(～非得做某事不可)」

I have to see a doctor.

我得去看個醫生。

Comics Businessman Zombie Tom [1]

I have a terrible hangover.

宿醉好不舒服啊。

⇒ hangover
宿醉

I have a splitting headache.

我覺得頭痛得快裂開了。

You have no choice but to do it.

就算是這樣，也別無選擇囉。

I've had enough of having this conversation.

話說，這段對話已經夠了。

⇒ have a headache
頭痛
⇒ have no choice but to ～
沒有～之外的選擇

I'm off to work.

我會去公司。

⇒ have had enough
已經對～覺得很煩
這是「have +過去分詞」的句型。莎曼珊的台詞有「（從過去到現在為止），這段對話已經說得太久」的意思。

⇒ (be) off to ～
朝向～

Have 的慣用句

湯姆發現變成殭屍的人

湯姆

Can I have a few words with you?

不好意思，可以借一步說話嗎？

I have no choice but to tell you.

我非得跟你說清楚不可。

Your face has some cracks.
You have only to look in the mirror.

你臉上有好幾處裂痕。
你只需要照照鏡子就會知道。

⇒ have only to ～
只需要做～

You had a hard experience.

你經歷了很糟的事情吧。

⇒ experience
經歷、體驗

Look! We have company.

看吧，有夥伴來了喲。

⇒ have company
有夥伴、訪客

傑克

交到殭屍朋友了

山姆

金彬

We are having a party this weekend.
我們這週末有派對喲。

I will have neat clothes on.
我會穿上漂亮的衣服。

But, I have nothing to do with you.
不過，我跟你沒什麼交情喲。

Have a good time.
請好好享受吧。

I have no friends.
我沒有朋友。

Survival Talk

You have me there! 你問倒我了啊！（我不知道）
→ 被對方問得團團轉的時候就用這句話吧！

015

Basic Verb 2

Go

湯姆總算上班去

go-went-gone/goes/going

①「去」 ②「be going to + 原形動詞（～準備做某事、預計做某事）
③「進行」 ④「成為～」 ⑤「離去、消失」

I can't find the time to go to my office.

可是我沒時間去公司。

Is your stomachache gone yet?

你肚子痛不是已經不痛了嗎？

Column　想說「～去做某事」時，可以使用 go + -ing 的形式。

例如：**go shopping**「去買東西」、**go skiing**「去滑雪」、**go hiking**「去遠足」、**go jogging**「去慢跑」、**go dancing**「去跳舞」、**go fishing**「去釣魚」、**go singing**「去唱歌」等。

That tie really goes well with your suit.

我就說這條領帶跟西裝很配吧。

⇒ go well with ～
與～很配、很適合

I don't want to wear a gray suit.
我不太想穿灰色的西裝啊。

It's going to rain soon.

快下雨了吧。

Zombies hate rain.
殭屍很討厭下雨的啊。

Do you want to go with me?

妳也要一起去嗎？

Huh? I'm not going.

蛤？我才不去咧。

We have no time to lose.
You have to step on it!
我們沒時間可以浪費了啦，
快點出門啦！

動詞PAPAGO 〔Go〕

go有從說話者的位置「離開」的意思，大致可分成①往其他的地方去（移動）、②去到看不見的地方（消失）、③從現在的地點前進（預計）等三種方向性的思考。其他還有be going to～「預計做某事」這類非動詞的使用方法。I've got to go.一般是「我非去不可」的意思，但有時候會是「我得去一下洗手間」的意思，所以go可說是使用方法非常多變的動詞。

變成殭屍後，去購物中心吧！

①「去」

We are ready to go.

我已經準備好出門了喲。

②「be going to + 原形動詞
（～準備做某事、預計做某事）」

Your organs aren't going to work anymore.

你的器官已經沒什麼用了吧。

⇒organ
器官

③「進行」

Everything's going as planned.

所有的事情都如預期進行中。

④「成為～」

Your skin went brown.

你的皮膚變成褐色了耶。

⑤「離去、消失」

Is your headache gone too?

頭痛已經不痛了嗎？

We are going to the shopping mall.

我們準備去購物中心。

Comics Businessman Zombie Tom [2]

I must be going now.
時間到了，我得快點去了。

Go ahead.
快去。

Tell me what's going on.
告訴我發生了什麼事。

⇒ go on
發生某事

⇒ won't go
無法正常運作

The car won't go.
車子怎麼都發不動。

**You can't drive a car.
You're a zombie!**
你不是沒辦法開車？
你忘了你是殭屍啊！

You're right!
對喔！

Survival Talk

go ahead　你先請、開始、往前進

→Go ahead, make my day. 是由克林伊斯威特飾演主角的知名電影《緊急追捕令》中，主角廣被流傳的台詞，有「繼續啊，我等著。」的意思。

Go 的慣用句

 我好像被公司
開除了

湯姆　　　　　　　　　　　　老闆

 The company decided to let you go.

公司決定要開除你。

⇒ decide　　⇒ let go
　決定　　　放手、解雇

 I won't go into this in detail.

我沒打算跟你詳細解釋。

 I'll go over the details of my life once more.

我會進一步思考我自己的人生。

⇒ go over ～
　進一步思考、調查某事

 I'm going to try again.

我打算再試試看。

 Tom, I will let it go this time.

湯姆，這次就先放手吧。

老闆

⇒ let it go
　放著不管、維持現在這樣
　那首知名歌曲《Let it go. 做自己》完全是意譯吧。

020

做了一個
流落街頭的夢

湯姆

My company went bankrupt.

公司破產了。

⇒ go bankrupt
破產

My savings are all gone.

存款全沒了。

The bread went moldy.

麵包發霉了。

⇒ moldy
發霉

My hair went grey from worry.

我擔心得頭髮都變白了。

⇒ go on a date
去約會

Would you go on a date
with poor little me!?

請跟可憐的我去約會。

Just what are
you dreaming
about?

現在是做了什麼
夢啊？

Basic Verb 3
Take

僵屍的上班之路

take-took-taken/takes/taking

①「帶去」 ②「取得、抓住」 ③「接受、接納；罹患疾病」
④「搭乘（大眾交通工具）」 ⑤「耗費（時間）」 ⑥「吃（藥）、放入；測量」
⑦「理解、認為」 ⑧「忍耐、承受」 ⑨「舉辦」

How long does it take to go to your company?

到你的公司要花多久時間呢？

It takes about one hour to get there.

到公司大概要花1個小時喔。

We're home!

我們回來了！

We took a walk around here.

我們剛剛在這附近散步。

⇒ take a walk
散步

Me?
我？

What should we do now?

那我們接下來該怎麼辦？

Could you take them to your company?

能幫我把他們帶去你的公司嗎？

023

基本中的基本動詞 Top10　[Take]　　　　　　　　　3/10

　　Take算是非常頻繁使用的動詞，因此除了「帶去」與「取得」這兩個基本用法外，翻開字典，居然可以找到28種之多的用法，可說是意義變化多端的動詞。I'll take this 的意思是「我要買這個」之外，take也可用在「耗費（時間）」這類說法，例如：He is taking forever to finish his work.「他總是花很多時間結束工作」就是其中一例。

你也一起成為殭屍吧！

①「帶去」

I'll take you to the grave.

讓我帶著你去墳墓吧。

②「取得、抓住」

He took me by the hand.

他抓住我的手。

⇒ take ～ by the hand
抓住～的手

③「接受、接納；罹患疾病」

I can't take your offer this time.

這次我無法接受你的提議。

④「搭乘（大眾交通工具）」

Let's take a carriage to the cemetery.

搭乘馬車去墓地吧。

⑤「耗費（時間）」

It won't take long.

不會耗費太多時間喲。

⑥「吃（藥）、放入；測量」

First, let me take your pulse.

首先，讓我測量一下你的脈搏吧。

⑦「理解、認為」

No pulse. What do you take this condition for?

沒有脈搏耶，你怎麼理解這個狀況呢？

⑧「忍耐、承受」

I can't take the pressure any more.

我無法忍受更多的壓力了。

No way. Don't take it too seriously.

不會吧。請不要太認真看待。

⑨「舉辦」

Your examination will take place at four o'clock.

看診會在4點的時候開始喲。

Your body has been taken over by the zombie virus!

你感染了殭屍病毒了！

錢德

丹尼爾

⇒ **take place**
舉辦

⇒ **take over**
占據

Column take+名詞 可用來表達很多種意思。

例如：**take a walk**「散步」、**take a bath**「洗澡」、**take a shower**「淋浴」、**take a rest[break]**「稍微休息一下」、**take a look at**「看一下～」、**take a train[bus, taxi]**「搭乘電車（公車、計程車）」等。

Survival Talk

You can take it as a joke.
你可以想成被開了一個玩笑。

→ 話說，要是被殭屍咬了，可就笑不出來了。

Take 的慣用句

Comics Businessman Zombie Tom [3]

I have to take care of them.

意思是，我得照顧這些傢伙啊。

⇒ take care of ～
照顧～

It takes a lot of time.

而且，又很花時間。

⇒ take time
花時間

Even though I have to take part in a meeting.

即使我待會兒還得參加會議。

⇒ even though
即使

⇒ take part in ～
參加～

I take it for granted that I go to work.

我認為去上班，是理所當然的。

I'll just leave them there.

就把這些傢伙丟在這裡吧。

⇒ take ～ for granted
視～為理所當然

請人接手照顧殭屍

瑪娜

年輕人

Could you take over my job?

你可以接手我的工作嗎？

⇒ take over ～
接手

I'll take that job.

我會接下這個工作。

Take care not to catch a zombie virus.

那你要小心，別感染殭屍病毒。

⇒ take care not to ～
～小心，別～

I take back my words.

我收回剛剛那句話。

⇒ take back
取消

No problem. Don't take your eyes off the zombie.

別擔心。
不要把視線從殭屍身上移開就好。

⇒ take one's eyes off ～
從～移開視線

Bye!

bring 與 take 的差異 ☞ p.186

027

Break

在公司受傷

break-broke-broken/breaks/breaking

《及物動詞》①「破壞～（打破、折斷、打碎等動作）」②「打破（規則、約定等抽象事物）」
③「坦白（不太好的事情）」
《不及物動詞》④「壞掉（破掉、斷掉、碎掉等狀況）」⑤「突破、克服」

莎耶

Can you lend me a hand?

你可以幫我一下嗎？

⇒ Could I have a hand?
這句也很常用

I have some bad news to break.

我有一些壞消息不知道該不該坦白。

⇒ bad news
壞消息

I broke my leg accidentally.

我不小心折斷了我的腿。

But, I know he broke his leg on purpose.

不過，我知道他是故意折斷自己的腳。

⇒ on purpose
故意地、別有企圖

Come now, losing his leg nearly broke him.

算了吧，他都因為斷了腳而這麼沮喪了。

Would you stop coming over to break in on our talk?

你能不能不要突然插嘴啊？

⇒ break in
插嘴

break up 變成一盤散沙、分手

Survival Talk

We broke up already. Didn't you know it?

我們不是已經分手了嗎？你不知道嗎？

→完全不知道什麼時候變成前男友的。真遺憾。

打破了那個女孩的杯子

《及物動詞》①「破壞~（打破、折斷、打碎等動作）」

I broke her cup accidentally.

我不小心打破她的杯子。

②「打破（規則、約定等抽象事物）」

You broke her rules.

你破壞了她的規則呢。

③「坦白（不太好的事情）」

I don't know how I will break the news to her.

我實在不知道該怎麼跟她坦白那件事啊。

《不及物動詞》④「壞掉（破掉、斷掉、碎掉等狀況）」

That cup broke into pieces.

那個杯子摔成碎片。

⑤「突破、克服」

Whew. Should we break through or run away?

糟了，是該突破，還是逃跑呢？

Whew. 咻（受到驚嚇的時候）。感嘆詞還有很多，請視情況使用。
Huh. 蛤？（是殭屍嗎？口吻較輕的質問）、Oops. 哎呀（是殭屍啊！驚訝）
Oh my. 搞砸了（感染了啊。失望的時候）
Sigh. 嘆氣（就當自己是殭屍活下去吧。那隻超級米格魯神犬布丁也常這麼說）。

Column break是**及物動詞**（需要受詞），也是**不及物動詞**（不需要受詞）。

《及物動詞「破壞~」》**break a window**「打破窗戶」、**break the law**「違反法律」、**break the speed limit**「違反速限」。

《不及物動詞「壞掉」》**The car broke.**「車子故障了」、**The day broke.**「天亮了」、**My arm broke.**「我的手臂骨折了」、**My heart broke.**「我的心碎了」。

Comics Businessman Zombie Tom [4]

I broke my wrist while I was working.

我剛剛在工作的時候手腕折斷了。

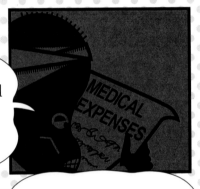

I'm broke. I wish medical expenses were cheaper.

我沒有錢，真希望醫藥費可以便宜一點。

I broke my leg, too. I'm flat broke.

腳也折斷了，身上又沒有半毛錢。

⇒ flat broke
身無分文

You should break through this situation.

你應該想辦法克服這個狀況。

Break 的慣用句

課長變成殭屍了

湯姆

The management chief's voice is beginning to break.

課長的聲音開始變了。

⇒ *one's* voice breaks
聲音改變

Sweat broke out all over his face.

他的臉冒了好多汗。

His glasses broke on the floor.

他的眼鏡掉在地板上，摔破了。

He broke down in tears.

他大聲哭了起來。

He broke into a laugh.

他突然噗哧地笑了出來。

⇒ 也可以說成 burst into ～

Zombie life is fun, too.
殭屍生活也很有趣喲。

課長

很難破除
對殭屍的偏見

秋霞小姐

阿玉小姐

Someone broke into my house.

有人闖進我家了呢！

⇒ **break into ～**
入侵、突然開始某事～、準備（金錢或備用品）

Really? A fire broke out near my house.

真的嗎？剛剛我家附近有火災耶。

⇒ **break out**
發生暴動或火災、冒出（疹子或是汗水）、脫逃

A number of cars broke down on the road.

有很多車在路上拋錨啦。

Well, a zombie broke out near my house.

話說回來，我家附近出現殭屍耶。

It's very hard to break through this prejudice.

要打破這種偏見還真難。

⇒ **break through**
克服、重大發現

⇒ **prejudice**
偏見

Basic Verb 5
Get

主管的壓力

get-got-got[gotten]/gets/getting

① 「得到、持有」　② 「帶來」　③ 「購買」　④ 「理解」　⑤ 「到達」
⑥ 「get +形容詞」→ 「成為～」　⑦ 「get +現在分詞」→ 「開始做～、做～」
⑧ 「get +過去分詞」→ 「被～」
⑨ 「get +受詞+ to不定詞」→ 「讓某人做某事、請某人做某事」

I don't get along well with my boss.

我跟老闆處得不好。

⇒ **get along**
相處

I'm under a lot of pressure from my boss.

老闆總是給我很大的壓力。

⇒ **under pressure**
承受壓力

034

Let's get down to business, everybody.

大家，準備開始工作吧。

⇒ **get down to ~**
準備開始某事

I get tired easily these days.

最近很容易感到疲勞。

⇒ **get tired**
感到疲勞

I want to get back home by four.

希望4點之前可以回家。

⇒ **get back**
回去～

I got through with my day's work.

我結束今天的工作了。

⇒ **get through with ~**
結束某事

It's still morning!

現在還是上午！

動詞PAPAGO〔Get〕

基本中的基本動詞 Top10　[Get]　　　　　　　　　　4/10

　　Get的基本用法是「取得」，而且不一定是取得東西，也有可能是「取得某種狀態」，其他的用法也很多，例如：get a letter「收到信件」、get a T-shirt「買T恤」、get $100「賺到100美元」、get the feeling that...「有～的感覺」、I got you.「我聽懂你想說的了（我取得你的想法了）」等。只要先掌握「取得」這個概念，就不難理解Get的用法。

老闆要開除我

① 「得到、持有」

I've got a bad feeling about this.

這件事讓我有不好的預感。

② 「帶來」

Relax. I'll get you a cup of coffee.

冷靜下來，我替你拿來咖啡吧。

③ 「購買」

I'm going to get a fresh human brains burger, too.

我也會買用人類新鮮腦漿做的漢堡喔。

④ 「理解」

I got it all wrong. You're already a zombie.

我整個理解錯誤了，你已經是殭屍了吧。

⑤ 「到達」

How can I get to the hamburger shop?　　　　　⇒ get to ～
抵達～

該怎麼去到漢堡店呢？

Column　get除了 get + 受詞 的「得到～」這種用法外，還有 get + 形容詞 以及「讓某人做某事」的使役型用法。

「get + 形容詞」：get dark「變暗」、get angry「變得生氣」、get ready「準備」。

「get 的使役型用法」：get him to come to the meeting「讓他參加會議」、get him to sign the agreement「讓他簽署同意書」。

036

⑥「get +形容詞」→「成為～」

I get hungry all the time.

我總是覺得肚子很餓。

⑦「get +現在分詞」→「開始做～、做～」

Let's get going.

差不多該去囉。

⑧「get +過去分詞」→「被～」

I almost got fired.

我剛剛差點被開除耶。

⑨「get +受詞+ to不定詞」→「讓某人做某事、請某人做某事」

Finally, I got my boss to understand me.

我總算讓老闆了解我的想法了。

I got a pay raise last month.
上個月加薪了。

Tom, get up!
湯姆，快起來！

⇒ **get up**
站起來、起床
cf. wake up
醒來

Survival Talk

Get off me! 別碰我！

→ 被殭屍襲擊時，請立刻說出這句話！若只是說Don't touch me！有可能
還是會被攻擊喔。

Get 的慣用句

女朋友是虛擬偶像

雅思

湯姆

I got an e-mail from her yesterday.

昨天我收到女朋友的信了。

You really got into Miki.

你真的很喜歡蜜琪耶。

⇒ get into ～
對～有興趣、沉迷

Miki and I got closer.

蜜琪跟我變得感情很好。

⇒ get closer
變得親近、感情好

We will get married in September.

我們打算9月結婚。

⇒ get married
結婚

Miki is a virtual idol.
蜜琪是虛擬偶像。

雅思

蜜琪

Maybe, he will get on the Internet tonight.

大概,他今晚也會上網吧。

Comics Businessman Zombie Tom [5]

Getting some sleep is way better than working.

稍微睡一下，會比一直工作好喔。

⇒ get some sleep
稍微睡一下

I see. Let's get back to work. Do you get it?

我知道了，回去工作吧。聽懂了嗎？

⇒ get it
理解

I'm afraid I don't.

我恐怕沒聽懂。

⇒ I'm afraid ...
很可惜「很不巧」…

What are you getting at?

你到底想說什麼？

⇒ be getting at ∼
暗示∼

OK. I got the point of it.

原來如此，我抓到重點了。

I remembered you are my boss.

我想起來，你是我的老闆這件事了。

Basic Verb 6
Do

莎耶的請求

do-did-done/does/doing

① 「做某事、做某物」→ 「do +名詞」do business, etc.
② 「帶來～、影響」→ do you good[harm], etc.
③ 「適合、足夠」

What shall I do?
Time for lunch.

我該做什麼啊？午餐時間了。

Do as you please.

隨你高興。

---

do over 重做一次

I mad another mistake. I'll do it over. 我又搞錯了。我會重做一次。

→ 要是失敗三次，丟句「This problem has nothing to do with me.」
（這問題跟我沒關係）就離開吧。

→ have nothing to do with～「與～沒有關係。」

Survival Talk

040

But, I'm not happy with your way of doing business.

可是，我不太滿意你的工作方式。

⇒ **way of doing business**
工作方式

Do you mean to say I don't do my duty?

妳是說，我沒有盡到工作責任嗎？

⇒ **do** *one's* **duty**
稱職

This is all your work. What are you going to do?

這些都是你的工作。你打算怎麼辦？

I'll do it right now.

我立刻做這些工作。

動詞PAPAGO 〔Do〕

基本中的基本動詞 Top10　[Do] 5/10

　　do是非常好用的動詞，只要在後面接上名詞，對方大概就知道你想要表達的意思（do lunch[a meeting, a movie]「吃午餐[開會、去看電影]」）。do的意思非常多，例如：I can do without you.「沒有你，我也可以做」、Be careful, or they'll do you.「小心點，否則他們就會騙你喲」、I can do Mr. Trump.「我可以模仿川普先生喲」。要是能活用do的用法，就能把英語說得很有趣。

工作永遠做不完

①「做某事、做某物」
What shall I do today?
今天要做什麼？

Do your work right now.
給我立刻開始做工作。

②「帶來～、影響」
This will do nothing for my job.
這對我的工作無濟於事。

③「適合、足夠」
That will never do.
這樣絕對不行「不夠」喲。

⇒ ～ will do
　足夠

> **It has nothing to do with me.** ☞ p.40
> 跟我沒有關係啦。

⇒ do nothing
沒有任何影響

> **I'm doing badly so far.**
> 到目前為止，都（做得很差）不順利啊。

Column　do用在「做」工作或家事時，可說成 do the -ing。如果要說「～結束了」，則可改用 done。

「**do the -ing**」：do the washing「洗衣服」、**do the job hunting**「找工作」。
「**be done**」：The report is done.「報告寫好了」。

042

Comics Businessman Zombie Tom [6]

What are you doing?

你在幹嘛？

I'm doing some research.

我正在查資料。

⇒ **do research**
查資料

Do you want me to help with your work?

要我幫忙嗎？

**I promise
I will do my best.**

我發誓，我會盡全力的。

⇒ **do *one's* best**
盡全力

Do 的慣用句

莎耶

湯姆不想工作

湯姆

What do you suggest I do this afternoon?

我下午做什麼比較好呢？

⇒ 請對方提供建議時的問法

I can't do anything for you.

我不能替你做任何事喔。

How can I do away with my work?

該怎麼解決工作呢？

⇒ do away with
廢止、去除、解決

It's time we do something about him?

該是時候幫他做點什麼了？

⇒ do something about
做點～、處置～

交給莎耶

莎耶

老闆

Let me do **his work.**

讓我做他的工作。

Here, I did **a good job.**

看吧,我做得很好吧。

⇒ **do a good job**
做得很好 (也可用於工作之外的情況)

She is doing well **at work.**

她總是把工作做得很好。

⇒ **do well**
做得很好

What should we do with **Tom?**

我們該拿湯姆怎麼辦?

We'll do without **Tom!**

就跳過湯姆,繼續做下去吧!

⇒ **do without ～**
在沒有～的情況下解決

Tell

「說話的動詞」Tell、Say、Talk、Speak
（說話、傳達）

客戶的祕密

tell-told-told/tells/telling

① 「說話、傳達」 ② 「要求～、命令」
③ 「（廣播、電視）報導」 ④ 「分辨」

To tell you the truth ...

老實跟你說……。

⇒ To tell (you) the truth ...
老實說

Please tell me straight even if it's difficult to say.

就算有苦衷，也請直說。

⇒ tell *one* straight
對某人直說

肯先生

I've been told not to trust dishonest people like you.

有人告誡我，不要相信你這種不老實的傢伙。

⇒ tell ～ not to ...
要求某人別做某事

Could you tell me who said that to you?

你可以告訴我，是誰跟你這麼說的嗎？

My mother told me.

我媽跟我說的啊。

I'll tell her not to say it again.

我會提醒她，別再說那樣的話。

Survival Talk

Don't tell me! 不會吧！

Don't tell me! Are you a zombie? 不會吧！你是殭屍？

→被殭屍咬的時候，就這麼說吧。

Time will tell.（時間會說明一切）聽到這句話，就確定是殭屍無誤。

身不由己

①「說話、傳達」

I told my wife that I became a zombie.
我告訴老婆我變成殭屍的事了。

②「要求～、命令」

She told me to sit down on the sofa.
她要求我坐在沙發上。

⇒ tell ～ to ...
要求某人做某事

③「（廣播、電視）報導」

The TV told of a zombie outbreak in the area.
電視上剛剛報導，這地區出現很多殭屍。

④「分辨」

Can you tell who that is over there?
你可以分辨在那裡的是誰嗎？

⇒ can tell (that) ...
分辨…

Why aren't you going there?
為什麼你不去那裡呢？

say	不需要有聽眾，單純說話 ☞ p.58
speak	不需要有聽眾，單純單方面發言 ☞ p.172
talk	需要有聽眾，是雙向溝通 ☞ p.88
tell	需要有聽眾，告訴對方內容（傳遞）（傳達）☞ p.46

Comics Businessman Zombie Tom [7]

**Don't tell anyone about this.
I like Fiona very much.**

這件事別跟任何人說喔。
我超喜歡費歐娜的。

You're telling me.

你沒這麼說我也知道啦。

You never can tell with love.

戀愛永遠是難以捉摸的啊。

⇒ you never can tell/
you can never tell
永遠不知道會發生什麼事

**But, it's very hard to tell
Fiona from her father.**

不過,要分辨費歐娜跟她爸爸,
可是很難的喔。

⇒ tell ~ from ...
辨別~與~

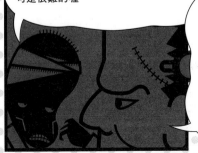

**You know I'm a client,
right?**

你應該知道,我是你的客戶吧?

**Can you tell me more
about it?**

你能不能多告訴我這些事?

客戶的八卦

 湯姆

 莎耶

I'll tell you all about it.

有關那件事，我會全說出來。

I'll tell you what. Mr. Ken likes Fiona very much.

請你稍微聽一下。肯先生超喜歡費歐娜喔。

But, I can't tell Fiona from her father.

可是，我無法分辨費歐娜跟她的爸爸。

Can you tell who that man is over there?

你知道站在那裡的男性是誰嗎？

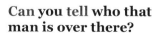

湯姆惹怒肯先生了

老闆

湯姆

Could you tell me what happened to you both?

請告訴我，你們兩個發生了什麼事。

Time will tell.

時間會說明一切。

Nobody can tell what may happen tomorrow.

世事總是難料啊！（誰也不知道明天與意外哪個先到。）

Tell me what's going on here?

快告訴我，（這裡）到底發生了什麼事？

Hey Boss. It's a call from Mr. Ken.

老闆，肯先生的來電。

He is very angry.
他超級生氣的。

Set

業務會議

set-set-set/sets/setting

① 「配置、放置」　② 「制定、劃定、朝向」　③ 「設定、決定」
④ 「使某人做某事」　⑤ 「轉化成某種狀態」

Let's set aside all formality today.

今天就把那些煩人的事放在一旁吧。

⇒ set aside
　放在一旁、暫不理會

set up

→set up a shout 放聲大叫　　set up a flag 立起旗幟
set up a tent 搭帳蓬　　set up a diversion 設立迴轉道
set up 有很多有利於殭屍恐慌的婉轉說法。

This novel is set in the Victorian era.

這部小說是以維多利亞女王時代為舞台的喲。

⇒ **be set in** ～
以～為舞台

She set some flowers in a vase.

她把花插在花瓶了。

That vase is out of style.

那個花瓶很土氣耶！

⇒ **out of style**
土氣

Excuse me, have you set up the sales meeting?

呃～業務會議的準備完成了嗎？

⇒ **set up** ～
準備～、設置～

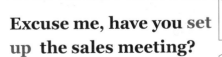

燒掉重要會議的文件

①「配置、放置」

The management chief set the document on the table.

課長把文件放在桌上。

⇒ set ~ on ...
　放～放在…

②「制定、劃定、朝向」

The members set their sights on the document.

與會人員紛紛轉向文件。

⇒ set *one's* sight on ~
　對準某個目標、設定基準

③「設定、決定」

Let's set a date for the next meeting.

決定下次開會的日期吧。

④「使某人做某事」

The management chief set upon them to write reports.

課長要他們寫報告。

⑤「轉化成某種狀態」

Saya set the document on fire.

莎耶在文件點火。

⇒ set ~ on fire
　在～點火

What documents?
這都是些什麼文件？

Comics Businessman Zombie Tom [8]

⇒ **be set for the meeting**
開會的準備沒問題了

Is everything set for today's meeting?
今天的會議都準備好了嗎?

She set the portable gas stove on the table.
她把卡式爐放在桌上。

He set the tableware on the table.
他把餐具排在桌上。

Tell me what you are setting for here?
到底這裡是在準備什麼啊?

We'll set aside some time for a meeting, too.
我們也會保留足夠的開會時間喲。

Set 的慣用句

準備開會

老闆

OK, let's set about starting the meeting.

接下來就準備開會吧。

⇒ set about -ing
準備做某事

Tom set out in his mobile game.

湯姆開始玩手機遊戲。

⇒ set out in ～
開始（旅行、遊戲）、朝向（目的地）

They set forth their views on lunch.

他們對午餐各自呈述了意見。

⇒ set forth ～
呈述～

I set the members free.

我決定散會。（讓與會人員自由）

⇒ set ～ free
讓～自由

......

肯先生每天都想見費歐娜

湯姆

肯先生

The next meeting is set up for tomorrow.

下次開會就訂在明天吧。

He set off to where Fiona was waiting.

他往費歐娜的地方出發。

⇒ set off
出發

I think Mr. Ken will set up a date with Fiona.

我想，肯先生跟費歐娜約好要約會。

It seems like Mr. Ken has set his love policy.

肯先生似乎制定了追求的方針。

057

say-said-said/says/saying

① 「說話」　② 「say（that）～」→「說了那樣的事」
③ 「是這麼說的、有謠傳說」　④ 「（報紙、天氣預報）是這麼報導的」

What do you say to having a meal with us?

一起吃個飯意下如何？

⇒ **What do you say to -ing?**
一起做～，意下如何？

What do you have to say to Tom's offer?

你對湯姆的提議有什麼意見呢？

⇒ **What do you (have to) say to ～ ?**
你對～的看法？
你對～的意見？

Please say it directly to me.

難以啟齒的事也請直說。

What do zombies eat?

各位殭屍都吃什麼呢？

Could you say that again?

你可以再說一遍嗎？

Go ahead and open it.

請打開看看。

動詞PAPAGO〔Say〕

殭屍謠傳

① 「說話」

I won't say a word about it.

就那件事而言，我一句話也不會多說的。

② 「say (that)～」→「說了那樣的事」

I'm saying (that) you are responsible for that.

我的意思是說，責任在你身上。

⇒ **be responsible for～**
責任在～身上

③ 「是這麼說的、有謠傳說」

It is said (that) we are zombies.

有謠傳說我們是殭屍。

④ 「（報紙、天氣預報）是這麼報導的」

**The newspaper said
zombies eat brains.**

報紙報導，殭屍會吃人腦。

I found out
that it's true.
我知道那件事是事實。

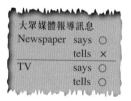

大眾媒體報導訊息		
Newspaper	says	○
	tells	×
TV	says	○
	tells	○

Survival Talk

You can say that again. 完全沒錯。

Are you saying we are zombies? You can say that again.

你是說，我們是殭屍？完全沒錯。

→要是聽到這句話，說不定已經沒機會逃跑了。

Comics Businessman Zombie Tom [9]

It goes without saying that he is a good zombie.

不用多說,他的確是個好殭屍。

⇒ **It goes without saying that**
那種事情不用多說

I can't make out what you're saying.

我無法理解你說的事情。

⇒ **make out**
理解、了解

I can't say he is a good zombie.

我無法斷言他是好殭屍喲。

What I want to say is that you'll understand one day.

我想說的是,總有一天你也會懂的。

⇒ **What I want to say**
我想說的是

Say 的慣用句

討厭殭屍的
錢德先生

錢德　　　　　　　　　湯姆

I'd like to say a few words.

請讓我說幾句話。

I must say I hate zombies.

要我說的話，我是討厭殭屍的。

It goes without saying that I'm a zombie.

不用多做解釋，我就是個殭屍。

☞ p.61

I can't say for sure, but you are also a zombie.

我不敢說得太絕對，
但你也已經是殭屍喏。

That's easy for you to say so.

別那麼輕易就把這件事說出口。

變成僵屍的
錢德先生

錢德

丹尼爾

I simply want to say you're really hungry.

我只是想說,你的肚子很餓吧。

What do you say to having some more brains?

要不要吃點人類大腦呢?

I wouldn't say no to another brain.

我很樂意享用另一個人腦。

⇒ wouldn't say no to ～
我對～不會說no(=不會拒絕)→樂意之至

Living right is easier said than done.

雖說要活得正直,但說得容易,要做很難。

say/speak/talk/tell的概念 ☞ p.48

063

look

「看的動詞」Look、See
（看、看起來）

被老闆眼線盯上

look-looked-looked/looks/looking

① 「看、看起來」　② 「look at的用法」→「看」　③ 「look at的用法」→「閱讀、調查、檢查」
④ 「look at的用法」→「思考、想」　⑤ 「看起來像～」

How do I look?

我看起來如何？（這個髮型）

⇒ **How do I look?**
我看起來如何？
不僅可用來問髮型，也
可用來問服裝或鞋子。

梅杜莎
（老闆眼線）

You look young for your age.

看起來比實際年齡年輕喲。

⇒ **for** *one's* **age**
以某人的年齡而言

That looks great on you.

非常適合妳。

Survival Talk

look different 看起來不一樣

You look totally different. 你看起來簡直若兩人。

→這句話可試著對畫好妝的女性或殭屍說說看喔。但應該都不會有好下
　場吧。

You always look out for yourself.

⇒ **look out for ～**
在意～

妳總是只在意自己的事情吧。

⇒ **look like ～**
看起來像～

You look a little chubby, but you don't need to look like a supermodel.

雖然看起來有點發福，
但也不需要看起來像是超級模特兒吧。

⇒ **chubby**
健康的發胖。如果想更客氣地說「有點發胖」，可使用plump這個單字。

Look into my eyes.

請看著我的眼睛。

⇒ **look into ～**
往～裡面看

I don't think you should stare at women.

不可以動不動就盯著女人看喲。

⇒ **stare**
盯著、凝視

動詞PAPAGO〔**Look**〕

無意間看到死人在路上走

① 「看、看起來」

If you looked carefully, you would have been able to find it.

如果更仔細看，就能發現了。

② 「look at的用法」→「看」

But, you looked at the walking dead.

不過，你看到的是在路上走的死者吧。

③ 「look at的用法」→「閱讀、調查、檢查」

Could I look at your body?

要不要檢查一下你的身體呢？

④ 「look at的用法」→「思考、想」

We need to look at this in various ways.

關於這件事，需要以各種方法思考。　　⇒ **various**
各式各樣的

⑤ 「看起來像～」

That rotten body looks great on you.

這腐爛的身體非常適合你。

⇒ **rotten**
腐爛的、腐敗的

殭屍研究員

Column　　使用look的時候，要特別注意 look+形容詞的「看起來像～」的用法，也要注意 look at～ 這種「看～」的用法。

「**look + 形容詞**」：**look happy[sad]**「看起來好像很開心 [難過]」、**look tired**「看起來很疲勞」、**look worried**「看起來很擔心」。

「**look at**」：**Look at the building !**「看那棟大樓！」、**They looked at the zombie.**「他們看到殭屍了。」

Comics Businessman Zombie Tom [10]

You look exhausted.

妳看起來累壞了。

⇒ **exhausted**
累壞、累趴了

Really? I wanted to look good while I'm working.

真的嗎？我希望工作的時候，
能看起來美美的耶。

You look just like a *Buddha*.

妳看起來跟佛祖一模一樣。

⇒ **look just like ～**
看起來與～一模一樣

Why are you angry? The Buddha's face looks radiant.

妳為什麼生氣？佛祖的臉看起來佛
光萬丈耶。

⇒ **radiant**
發出光輝

Look 的慣用句

尋找費歐娜的
肯先生

肯先生

湯姆

Mr. Ken is looking around restlessly.

肯先生不安地東張西望。

⇒ restlessly
躁動、不安

He is looking for Fiona.

他正在尋找費歐娜。

⇒ look for ～
尋找～

People often say Fiona looks like her father.

費歐娜常被說跟她爸爸看起來很像喲。

She and her father look totally different.

她跟她爸爸看起來完全不像喲。

see的概念是「看映入眼簾的東西」 ☞ p.106
look的概念是「視線或臉往東西的方向轉去的看」 ☞ p.64
watch的概念是「看著正在移動的物體的看」 ☞ 可惜本書沒介紹。

不要鄙視殭屍

梅杜莎　　　　　　　　　　　　錢德先生

How do I look as a zombie?

我看起來是怎麼樣的殭屍？

Look at me!

請看看我！

Do not look down on zombies.

不行鄙視殭屍喲。

When I look at you, you will turn to stone.

被我盯著，可是會變成石頭喲。

I'm not looking down on you.
我可沒有鄙視你喲。

069

Come

不期而遇

come-came-come/comes/coming

① 「來（往說話者在的地方或是說話者要去的地方）」
② 「去（對方在的地方或是對方要去的地方）」 ③ 「變成～」（come+形容詞）

I came across a senior colleague downtown.

在路上碰到公司的前輩。

What are you doing here?
你在這裡做什麼？

⇒ **come across**
偶然碰見

⇒ **colleague**
同事

Please come this way.

請妳來這邊一下。

Survival Talk

come up with an idea 想到某個點子

I came up with a few ideas to escape！
我想到幾個脫逃的點子喔！
→第一個點子會失敗，第二個也有可能不會成功。

Come a little closer. I have something important to tell you.

請再靠過來一點，我有非跟妳說的大事。

I like your shoes.

你的鞋子很好看耶。

How silly you are!

你在說什麼傻話啊！

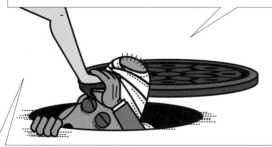

Come to the subway station with me.

請跟我一起去地下鐵的車站。

No way! Do you think I'd go through such a hole?

不可能！你以為我會跟你從這個洞去嗎？

動詞PAPAGO〔**Come**〕

基本中的基本動詞 Top10　[Come]

　　Come這個動詞的基本用法雖然是「來」，但有時會出現「去」的用法，使用上要特別小心（→Column）。此外，come+形容詞「變成～」的用法也非常重要，請大家務必熟記，例如My dream came true.「我的夢想實現了」、Everything came out right.「所有事情都一帆風順」、The dead came alive.「死者復活了」（也有The broken computer came alive.「壞掉的電腦又動起來了」的用法）。

殭屍去了又來

①「來（往說話者在的地方或是說話者要去的地方）」

Here come the zombies.

殭屍們會來這裡。

⇒ **The zombies come here.**
改變語順，藉此強調here「這裡」的說法

②「去（對方在的地方或是對方要去的地方）」

Are you coming to the Monroeville Mall?

要去蒙羅維爾購物中心嗎？

③「變成～」（come+形容詞）

Their dreams will come true someday.

他們的夢想總有一天會實現吧。

這裡是殭屍嚮往的購物中心。

MONROEVILLE MALL

Column　我們一起來認識come「來」當成「去」使用時，與go的「去」有什麼不一樣吧。go是離開自己的位置，往某個地方去的時候使用，但是**come卻是用於說明要去（接近、往）對方的位置時使用**。

I'm coming.「現在要去了（去對方的位置）」、

I'll come to your office at 10 tomorrow.「我明天10點會去你的公司拜訪」。

Comics Businessman Zombie Tom [11]

Would you like to **come** to the shopping mall with me?

要不要跟我一起去購物中心呢？

Wait a minute. Your shoelace **came** untied.

稍等一下，你的鞋帶鬆開了。

⇒ **come untied**
鬆開了

Nice kick!
You've **come** a long way.

踹得好，妳進步了耶。

⇒ **have come a long way**
經歷很多事情之後有所成長
You've come a long way, baby.
「妳成為好女人了啊，寶貝。」
會這麼說，代表你是個硬漢喔。

Come 的慣用句

在旅館遇到殭屍

金彬

飯店服務人員

Something's coming over.

好像有什麼往這邊過來。

⇒ **come over**
往這邊過來、往這邊接近

A big group of zombies is coming by this hotel.

一大群殭屍路過這間旅館。

⇒ **come by**
路過

When I shoot my gun, the bullets won't come out.

開了槍,子彈卻射不出來。

This broom will come in handy.

這枝掃把可能幫得上忙。

⇒ **come in handy**
幫得上忙

傑克與丹尼爾是朋友

丹尼爾　　　　　　　　　　　　　傑克

Actually, I came down with the zombie virus.

其實，我染上了殭屍病毒。

⇒ come down with ～
染上（感冒）

Oh, come on. I came down with the zombie virus, too!

喂，振作一點！我也染上殭屍病毒了啦！

Do you want to come along?

要一起來嗎？

Why don't you come over? Let's have intestines together.

要不要來我家玩？我們一起吃腸子。

⇒ come over
順道（去說話者的家）
來（吃飯）

I've never had it.
我從來沒吃過（腸子）耶！

Basic Verb 12
Try

前往會議途中

try-tried-tried/tries/trying

①「嘗試、努力」　②「試著做～」

I'm trying to keep in shape by working out at the gym.

⇒ **work out**
運動、重訓

我通常會在健身房重訓，努力維持體態。

Also, I'm trying to exercise by giving chase once a week.

而且會一週玩一次捉鬼遊戲，試著努力運動。

First, I try to find zombies.
第一件要做的事就是尋找殭屍。

I'm trying to catch Mana.

我試著抓住瑪娜。

⇒ **try to ～**
試著～

I'll try to eat your pancreas.

我會試著吃掉妳的胰臟。

**I don't think
I can help you.**

我不認為我能幫上你的忙喲。

**I tried and tried,
but it didn't go well.**

不管試了幾次,還是(吃)不到。

Try again next week.

請下週再試看看吧。

動詞PAPAGO 〔**Try**〕

瑪娜也想當殭屍

① 「嘗試、努力」

It wasn't very effective, so I tried another way.
這看起來效果不彰，所以我試了其他方法。

⇒ **effective**
有效的

② 「試著做～」

I tried persuading her, but it was all in vain.
我試著說服她，卻徒勞無功。

⇒ **in vain**
徒勞無功、無用的

try -ing	「（實際）試著做」
過去式 tried -ing	「（實際）試過了」
try to	「（有可能行不通）但還是試試看」
過去式 tried to	「試著做（結果行不通〔結果沒做〕）」

Try not to move your body.
請試著靜止不動。

⇒ **try not to ～**
試著不要做～

No way.
不可能。

Survival Talk

try out 嘗試

You should try out some zombie food!
請試試看殭屍食物！

→不是殭屍的話就不可以吃，不然算是違法喔。

Comics Businessman Zombie Tom [12]

I'm trying to find a restroom.
我正試著找洗手間。

Try visiting the city hall and you'll find one.
可以去市公所看看，應該會找得到吧。

I'm busy, so I'm going ahead.
我有急事，先走了。

⇒ **go ahead**
先離開  p.19

Zombies try to follow me everywhere.
殭屍總是試著如影隨形地跟著我。

He is a serious zombie.
他是個認真的殭屍。

被殭屍搭訕了

傑克

瑪娜

Will you try some zombie food tonight?

今晚要不要吃吃看殭屍料理?

I'm trying to stay away from high-calorie foods.

我是盡可能避吃高熱量的食物喲。

⇒ stay away from ~
不靠近、避開

I'm trying to remain calm at all times.

我總是試著讓自己保持平常心。

⇒ remain calm
保持平常心

Huh, is that how you see me?
蛤,原來你是那樣看我的啊?

湯姆嘗試增強體力

湯姆

瑪娜

I'm trying to get Mana.

我想追到瑪娜。

That's why I'm trying to work out at the gym.

基於這個理由，我試著在健身房重訓。

⇒ that's why ～
基於這個理由～

I tried on the training wear for size.

我試穿了訓練服，看看大小合不合適。

⇒ try on ～
試穿

I tried lifting the dumbbell, but it did not move.

我試著舉起啞鈴，
卻怎麼也舉不起來。

⇒ try -ing
試著做～

Work 工作完蛋了

work-worked-worked/works/working

① 「工作、讀書」　② 「運作、作動、運轉」
③ 「進展順利、有效」

**When I was working,
there was a blackout due to a
lightning strike.**

⇒ **blackout**
　停電
⇒ **due to ～**
　因為～原因而～、因為～
⇒ **lightning strike**
　閃電雷擊

工作時，突然打雷閃電，導致停電。

I lost four hours' worth of work.

做了4個小時的工作都白費了。

⇒ 「金額、時間、容量這類詞」+worth of ～，相當於是
「金額、時間、容量這類詞」的價值的～

My computer does not work correctly.

我的電腦無法正常運作。

Nothing seems to work out right for me.

我好像做什麼都不順利。

⇒ **correctly**
正確地、正常地

⇒ **work out (right)**
進展順利

Still, they make us work so hard.

而且我們一直被逼著工作。

⇒ **to start with**
首先～

To start with, you are not working at all.

首先要說的是，你根本沒在工作。

動詞PAPAGO〔**Work**〕

湯姆不適合這份工作

① 「工作、讀書」

You really work hard.

你真的很認真工作耶。

② 「運作、作動、運轉」

Your brain works so well today.

你的腦袋今天很清醒。

③ 「進展順利、有效」

That method is sure to work well.

照這樣下去，工作一定很順利。

> **So what?**
> 所以咧？

work overtime 加班

I don't like working overtime.

我不喜歡加班。

→這點我也一樣啦。

Comics Businessman Zombie Tom [13]

He works as a sales rep for my company.

他的工作是個業務員。

⇒ sales rep
業務員

I've done computer work for a long time and my computer won't work anymore.

長久以來都使用電腦工作，但我的電腦已經當掉了。

You could work instead of me.

你可以代替我工作啊。

⇒ instead of ～
～代替

Can you look after my work while I'm out?

我出門的時候，可以幫我看一下工作嗎？

His seat may be gone when he comes back.

他回來之後，這公司可能沒有他的容身之處了。

085

Work 的慣用句

 快工作，湯姆

湯姆

莎耶

How hard were you working?

你到底多拚命工作啊？

I was working on a difficult task.

我曾負責很難的工作。

⇒ **work on ～**
著手負責

It was supposed to work out well for me.

我原以為什麼事情應該都會順利。

⇒ **～ work out**
最終得到～的結果

⇒ **be supposed to ～**
成為～的現況

Didn't it work out that way?

結果不如預期嗎？

莎耶很認真工作

湯姆

莎耶

How about Friday the 20th at 11?
Does that work for you?

20日的星期五的11點如何？有配合你的時間嗎？

⇒ work for ～
於～有用

I'll try working on the task.

我會試著著手進行這件工作。

She has worked very hard to finish the task.

她總是拼命工作，去完成任務。

My brain was working so hard trying to fix the computer.

只要電腦修好，
我的大腦就會拼命運作。

⇒ work hard
拼命工作

Can someone just fire Tom!?
有人可以幫我開除湯姆嗎！？

087

Talk

「說話的動詞」Tell、Say、Talk、Speak
（說話）

拜訪客戶

talk-talked-talked/talks/talking

《不及物動詞》①「說話」 ②「演說、演講」 《及物動詞》 ③「說話」

What are we talking about in the meeting today?

今天的會議要談什麼呢？

⇒ talk about ～
針對～談論

We hope to talk to your company about a new project.

想就新專案跟你們公司談談。

⇒ talk to ～
與～談談、說話

I talked very slowly.

我會說得非常慢。

What is he talking about?

他剛剛說什麼？

By the way, you'll be talked about if you're always gazing at Fiona.

話說回來，聽說你最近眼裡只有費歐娜啊。

⇒ be talked about
被謠傳、被評論

⇒ gaze at ～
凝視～、盯著～不放

Who is Fiona?

費歐娜是誰？

說出事實

《不及物動詞》①「說話」

He talks a lot.
他是個愛說話的人。

I know what I'm talking about.
我很清楚自己在說什麼。

②「演說、演講」

Tom talked about some zombies' love situation.
湯姆針對殭屍的戀愛方式演說。

《及物動詞》③「說話」

Don't talk nonsense.
可以不要隨口亂說嗎？

I just talked about the truth.
我只是說出事實。

Tom often talks back to me.
湯姆常常頂嘴。

⇒ talk back
頂嘴

say/speak/talk/tell的概念 ☞ p.48

Survival Talk

talk ~ out of -ing 努力說服～，讓～放棄…

She's trying to talk the zombie out of eating her.
她正努力說服殭屍，放棄吃掉她。
→殭屍通常只會說英語，要是你不會說英語，就會被殭屍吃掉喔。

Comics Businessman Zombie Tom [14]

We talked the problems out together.

我們好好聊聊那個問題吧。

⇒ talk ~ out
好好聊聊~

Please stop talking about me.

可以不要再討論我嗎?

He often talks to himself.

他很常自言自語。

⇒ talk to *oneself*
自言自語

I am telling everyone.

我正在跟大家說。

Don't talk to me while I'm in a meeting.

開會時,別跟我搭話。

Talk 的慣用句

湯姆

講電話的時候，別跟我搭話

Please don't talk to me.

請不要跟我搭話。

⇒ talk to ～
某一方與另一方「搭話」的語氣

I'm talking on the phone at the moment.

我現在正在講電話。

⇒ at the moment
當下、現在

Who are you talking to on the phone?

你在跟誰講電話？

I have to talk with my wife about dinner.

我必須先跟老婆商量晚餐的事。

⇒ talk with ～
一來一往對話的語氣

正在聊肯先生的八卦

肯先生　　　　　　　　湯姆

Talking about Mr. Ken, he seems like he went on a date with Fiona.

說到肯先生，他好像跟費歐娜約會了。

⇒ talking about ～　　⇒ seem like ～
說到～　　　　　　　貌似～

You talk a lot.

你真的很大嘴巴耶。

I don't want other people to hear what I'm talking about.

我討厭被別人聽到我講的事情。

You talk too loud. It is disturbing the whole room.

你說話的聲音太大了，整個房間都是你的聲音，很吵耶。

⇒ loud　　　　　⇒ disturb
音量很大　　　　干擾、妨害

Let

僵屍來襲

let-let-let/lets/letting

①「讓～做某事」(使役動詞)
②「以Let's～的語法使用」→「一起做什麼吧!」　③「轉換成～的狀態」

Excuse me!　Let me through.

不好意思,請讓我過去。

大衛

I will never let you down, so let me have a look at your intestines.

我一定不會讓妳失望的啲。
所以請讓我看看妳的內臟。

⇒ let ～ down
讓～往下、掉下、失望

Let's give it a try.

讓我試(吃)看看

⇒ **give it a try**
試著做看看

Go ahead.
Make my day!

請啊，
辦得到你就試試看啊！

▶ p.19

⇒ **go ahead**
你先請

⇒ **make my day**
辦得到就試試看啊！

Let me feel
your forehead.

讓我摸摸妳的額頭。

⇒ 也可當成「有沒有發燒」的意思使用

Don't make me
do this again!

滾開！別再讓我這麼做！

⇒ **make** ＋人＋原形動詞
強迫某人做某事

麥克

---

let out a long sigh 長長地嘆了一口氣

"A zombie's here…" Saya let out a long sigh.

「有隻殭屍來了……」莎耶長長地嘆了一口氣。

→儘管莎耶並不害怕，但普通人請放聲大叫（let out a cry）。

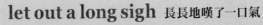

095

你也一起成為殭屍吧！

①「讓～做某事」（使役動詞）

Let me help with the meeting.
請讓我幫忙準備這個會議。

②「以Let's～的語法使用」→「一起做什麼吧！」

Let's not put off dealing with a problem.
別讓這個問題拖到後面才解決。

> ⇒ **put off**
> 延期、延後
> ☞ p.113

> ⇒ **deal with ～**
> 處理～、對應

Let's face the truth.
面對現實吧。

Let's not talk about it.
可以不要再談那件事了嗎？

③「轉換成～的狀態」

Could you let the blinds down?
可以讓百葉窗放下來嗎？

> **For the time being,
> let her handle it!**
> 這段期間就先交給她吧！

> ⇒ **for the time being**
> 當下、這段期間

> ⇒ **handle**
> 處理～、負責～

英雄J

Comics Businessman Zombie Tom [15]

**Let me tell you something.
I'm having a big crisis.**

請讓我說句話。我現在陷入重大危機了。

⇒ **crisis**
危機、緊急關頭

**Please let me ask
your advice.**

請讓我聽聽你的建議。

⇒ **ask *one's* advice**
請求～的建議

**Don't let me influence
your decision.**

請別讓我動搖妳的決心
（請別讓我影響你）。

⇒ **influence**　⇒ **decision**
影響　　　　決心、決定

Just let it be.

就這樣放著不管吧。

⇒ **let ～ be**
輕輕放下～、先放下～不管

Let 的慣用句

讓部下遭遇了危險

莎耶

老闆

I let her go there. A zombie attacked her there.

是我讓她去那裡的。殭屍在那裡襲擊她。

I won't let that happen again.

我絕對不會讓這種事情再次發生（絕不會再這麼做）。

I will let you off this time.

下不為例，這次就放過你。

⇒ let off ～
　　　放過～

Don't let me down.

別讓我失望喔。

Column　let當成「讓某人做某事」使用時，受詞後面的動詞請先恢復成原形。（這時候的用法與make、have相同）let有**「讓人如願做某事、允許某人做某事」**的意思。

例如：**I'll let you go home**.（我會讓你回家）、**Let me take a picture of you**.「請讓我替你拍張照片」。

雅思看醫生

雅思　　　　　　　殭屍研究員

Let me take your coat.

讓我幫你掛好外套。

Let's set aside all formality.

就別說什麼客套話了。

Could you let me have your fiancée's name?

可以讓我知道未婚妻的名字嗎？

⇒ let me have *one's* name
請告訴我～的名字

Miki? Let me have a look at the picture.

蜜琪？請讓我看看她的照片。

Let's say Miki is a human.

就假設蜜琪是人類吧。

⇒ let's (just) say (that)
就假設是～

Let's say? What are you talking about?

假設？你到底在說什麼啊？

099

Give

獵人頭

give-gave-given/gives/giving

①「給予」 ②「傳遞、告知」 ③「（源自給予的）做～某事」

When you have made up your mind to take the job, give me a call.

⇒ make up
one's mind
下定決心

決定接受這份工作的話，請給我電話。

Could you give me time to think it over?

請給我一點時間好好想想。

⇒ think ～ over
好好想想

Survival Talk

give out 發送

I heard they are giving out a zombie vaccine at the laboratory.

似乎有人正在研究所發送殭屍的疫苗。

→這可是致命的關鍵字，一定要記住喔。

Can you give me your ideas on that?

關於這點，請說說你的看法。

Giving me a doubled salary would be very appealing.

我覺得給我兩倍的薪水
是非常有吸引力的。

⇒ appealing
有吸引力的

I'm not happy with my company.

我對自己的公司不太滿意。

⇒ be happy with ～
對～滿意

I can give my consent to your plan!

我贊成你們的計畫！

⇒ give *one's* consent to ～
同意、承諾

Oh! Boss! There you are!

哇！老闆！你什麼時候在那裡的！

動詞PAPAGO〔Give〕

　　Give的基本用法為「無償的給予」，能給予的對象也不僅限於物品。例如：give a smile「給人一個微笑」、a chance「機會」、thanks「感謝」、satisfaction「滿足」都可作為give這個動詞的受詞。有格調的殭屍當然希望能給予自己的身體囉。

懇求老闆

①「給予」

Please give me one more chance.

請再給我一次機會。

②「傳遞、告知」

Let me give you an explanation about that.

請讓我說明那件事。

③「（源自給予的）做～某事」

I won't give you any excuse.

我不打算多做辯解。

Would you give me some advice?

能請您給我建議嗎？

Please give me a smile.

請給我一個微笑。

Please switch jobs, Tom.

湯姆，請換工作。

Column　give常常需要兩個受詞，也就是以 **give+人+物** 的語法使用。

I'll give him a chance of promotion.「我會給他一個升官的機會。」

I'll give you a ride.「我載你一程吧。」

I'll give her a call.「我會打電話給她。」

Comics Businessman Zombie Tom [16]

Your salary will be doubled.

你的薪水會變成兩倍。

I'll give it my best shot.

我會盡全力工作的。

⇒ give 〜 *one's* best shot
對〜盡全力

I'll give you more details about the project later.

之後請告訴我這個專案的細節。

OK! I always give in to you.

沒問題！我會永遠服從你的啲。

⇒ give in
投降、屈服

Oh! Boss!
There you are!

哇！老闆！
你什麼時候
在那裡的！

We'll be giving Tom a farewell party.

我們會給湯姆辦一個送別會。

⇒ farewell
送別、告別

I give a heartfelt apology.

我由衷地感到抱歉。

⇒ heartfelt apology
誠心誠意的道歉

Give 的慣用句

湯姆放棄跳槽了

湯姆

老闆

I gave up trying to change jobs.

我放棄跳槽了。

Don't give me trouble. You should find a new job.

別給我添麻煩,就說你應該跳槽了。

⇒ give ～ trouble
對～添麻煩

Please give my best regards to the CEO.

請幫我跟社長致上敬意。

⇒ give *one's* regards to ～
對～致上敬意

Don't give up.

別放棄(跳槽)啊。

You can do it!
Find a new job!

你一定可以的,就跳槽吧!

請幫忙（我）工作

莎耶

湯姆

My boss gave us permission.

老闆許可了。

⇒ give premission
許可

Then, can you give me a hand?

那，你能幫我一下嗎？

⇒ give a hand
幫手、幫忙

I'd like to give you the directions for this work.

我會給你指示，告訴你這件工作怎麼進行。

She gave me filing work.

她給我建檔的工作。

I'm giving up on work today.

今天的工作已經告一段落了啦。

⇒ give up on ～
看透～、放棄～

I'll never trust Tom ever again.

我再也不會相信湯姆了。

105

See

「看的動詞」Look、See
（看、看得見、參觀）

茶餘飯後

see-saw-seen/sees/seeing

①「看、看得見、參觀」　②「看某人做某事」　③「見面」
④「調查、確認」　⑤「理解」

I saw Tom arguing with the boss.

我看到湯姆正在跟老闆吵架喲。

⇒ argue
議論、吵架

I'll see what I can do about that.

我會想想看，
關於這件事我能做什麼。

Don't worry about it.

別煩惱那些事啦。

I can see Tom from here. He's sleeping.

從這裡可以看得見湯姆。他正在睡覺啊。

He should see a doctor.

他應該去給醫生看看才對。

Everyone here should see a doctor.

我們公司的每個人都應該
請醫生看看。

See you later.

那，待會兒見。

Here comes the boss.

老闆來了耶。

Survival Talk

I'll go and see it. 我會去看看。

可以在外面有殭屍聚集的時候說這句話。
→口語的話，通常會去掉and。

誰吃了杯麵？

①「看、看得見、參觀」
Have you seen my Royal instant noodles around here?
你有看到我的皇家泡麵？

②「看某人做某事」
I saw Tom buying a instant noodles at the drug store.
我有看到湯姆在雜貨店買泡麵。

③「見面」
I will see Tom later.
之後我會去見湯姆。

④「調查、確認」
I should see whether this information is right or not.
我應該確認這個資訊是否正確（會比較好吧）。

⇒ **whether ～ or not**
　　～是否

⑤「理解」
Do you see the point I'm making?
你了解我想說的重點嗎？

That's not mine.
這不是我的泡麵。

Comics Businessman Zombie Tom [17]

Shall we see a movie this weekend?
這個週末要不要去看電影？

Sorry! I've already got plans.
抱歉，我有約了。

By the way, do you often see Mr. Ken?
話說，妳最近很常跟肯先生見面？

I have heard a lot about Mr. Ken.
我聽了不少有關肯先生的傳聞。

⇒ **hear about ～**
仔細聽～

I'll see what I can do for Fiona.
我會想想看，我能為**費歐娜**做什麼。

Let's see about Fiona's love situation.
讓我們討論一下費歐娜的戀情吧。

⇒**see about ～**
針對某事討論「考慮」。

109

梅杜莎是時尚指標

梅杜莎

莎耶

I was surprised to see lots of people come to work in nice clothes.

每次看到別人穿得漂漂亮亮上班，都讓我好驚訝。

⇒ nice clothes
時髦的服飾

Seeing fashionable people makes me want to go shopping.

看到打扮時髦的人，就會想到去購物吧。

I can see that you are really cool.

我能了解你有多酷。

That makes sense. I see what you mean.

也是啦，我能理解。
我知道妳想說什麼。

⇒ make sense
有道理、講得通

look/see的概念 p.68

誰在準備會議

梅杜莎　　　　　　　　　　　　　　莎耶

Who's seeing to the preparations for the meeting this afternoon?

今天下午的會議是誰在準備？

⇒ see to ～
照顧～、處置～

That's Tom's role. I'll see to it that everything is ready.

是湯姆的任務。我會確認他是不是準備妥善。

⇒ see to it that ～　　　　⇒ role
確認～　　　　　　　　　任務、角色

We'll go and see if everything is OK.

快去，看看是不是一切就緒吧。

⇒ see if ～
確認是否沒問題

I saw Tom sleeping in the hallway.

湯姆的話，我看到他在走廊正在睡覺啦。

Do you see the point I'm making?
你懂我想說的事情吧？　　p.108

I'd like an office with a bedroom.
我希望在設有寢室的辦公室上班。

Put

湯姆與老闆的午後

put-put-put/puts/putting

①「放置」　②「轉換成某個狀態」　③「寫、說」

You're already putting your feet up on the desk.

We're still at work.
明明還在工作中。

你已經把腳放在桌子上了耶。

Please put yourself in my shoes. You are my boss.

請站在我的立場想看看。
你是我的老闆啊。

⇒ put yourself in *one's* shoes
直譯是「穿我的鞋子」,但其實是「站在～的立場想看看」的慣用句。

Survival Talk

put on a ~ attitude 裝成～的態度

Put on a zombie attitude. 裝成殭屍的態度.

→ 裝成殭屍有利於逃跑,請從平常就開始練習喲。

☞ p.118 也可以使用make believe (that)「裝成～的樣子」。

It's your job to think about what we do next.

思考下一步是你的工作吧。

OK! Can you put your name down here?

我知道了，你能在這裡寫下你的名字嗎？

⇒ **put down** ～
寫下～

As far as I'm concerned, this project should be put off.

就我而言，這件事應該要延期吧。

⇒ **As far as I am concerned**
就我而言、只要與我有關的

⇒ **put off**
延期、延後

He put that paper in the trash.

他把那張紙放進垃圾箱了。

⇒ **put ～ in the trash**
將～放進垃圾箱

I can't put up with days like this.

我無法忍受每天這樣。

⇒ **put up with** ～
忍耐～

put的基本用法為「放置」，但有時會有「塗抹、放入」的用法，建議大家一起背下來。put本來就有「將某物置於某處」的意思，所以將「文字」放在「紙上」就是「寫字」，不過要注意的是，這種說法與中文的不同之處在於放的不是東西，紙張也不是我們認知的放置的場所。此外，有許多諺語都會用到這個動詞，建議大家都一起背下來，就能把英語講得更生動喲。

整理桌面

①「放置」

I put that file on my desk, but I can't find it.

我明明把那個檔案放在我的桌上，現在居然找不到。

②「轉換成某個狀態」

I'll put my desk in order right now.

立刻來整理我的桌子吧。

③「寫、說」

I put down my boss's words.

先寫下老闆說的話。

To put it one way, he is a real blockhead.

簡單來說，他就是個遲緩的傢伙。

**To put it another way,
he is cunning.**

換句話說，他很精明。

Now, he is sleeping
under the desk.

所以，他現在躲在桌子底下睡覺。

Comics Businessman Zombie Tom [18]

**Let's put this plan into action.
Turn your paperwork in.**
讓我們開始執行這項計畫吧。請先提出書面資料。

**I can't remember
where I put it.**
我想不起來那份書面資料放在哪裡了。

⇒ put ～ into action
讓～開始執行

**I remember now!
I put it in the postbox.**
我想起來了，我把它放進郵筒了。

**Did you put a stamp
on the envelope?**
有在信封貼郵票嗎？

I forgot to put the stamp on.
我忘了貼郵票。

**The mail will
come back to me.**
郵件會回到手上吧。

**I want to put an end to my
relationship with Tom.**
我想跟湯姆斷絕關係。

⇒ put an end to ～
讓～結束

Put 的慣用句

山姆的殭屍料理

山姆

Put all of the beaten egg in there.

先將蛋液全部倒進去。

Could you please put away your messy hair?

請先整理凌亂的頭髮。

⇒ **messy hair**
凌亂的頭髮

Now, put out the fire.

好的，關火。

You have to put up with only three minutes to eat.

接著忍耐3分鐘就能吃了。

This dish is delicious, so I've put on 10 pounds.

這料理太好吃了，我胖了10磅。

⇒ **put on ～ pound(s)**
體重增加了～磅

116

老闆提出新企畫

老闆

莎耶

The boss put forward a new plan.

老闆提出新的企畫了。

⇒ **put forward**
提案

Tom stopped reading the magazine and put it aside to read the new plan.

湯姆沒繼續閱讀雜誌，而是先把雜誌放在一旁，讀了企畫書。

⇒ **put ~ aside**
將～放在一旁

The plan put Tom to sleep.

那份企畫書讓湯姆睡著了。

⇒ **put ~ to sleep**
讓（使）入睡

I would like to put Tom on the market.

我想賣掉湯姆。

⇒ **put ~ on the market**
賣掉～、把～放到市場

I'd never buy him.
我絕對不會買他。

117

Make

湯姆的視察

make-made-made/makes/making

① 「製作；預備、準備」 ② 「讓某事發生」
③ 「讓～轉換成某種狀態」 ④ 「讓某人做某事」（使役動詞）

I'm glad you could make it.

你能來我很開心。

⇒ make it
參加、出席（會議或活動）

Have you made plans for the inspection?

視察的計畫做好了嗎？

⇒ make a plan
訂定計畫

Of course, we will really make it big.

當然，一定會非常成功。

⇒ make it big
非常成功

Survival Talk

make believe (that) 假裝～的樣子

He made believe he was a zombie.
他假裝成殭屍的樣子。

→很像是在開玩笑，一旦被識破的話，可是會被吃掉喔。 ☞ p.112

That's amazing! I'd like to make a phone call.

這個好厲害！只是我想打個電話。

⇒ **make a (phone) call**
打電話

The company will make an announcement about it tomorrow.

公司明天會發表這件事吧。

⇒ **make an announcement**
發表

This doesn't make sense!

我不知道這有什麼意義！

⇒ **make sense**
了解意思、
能夠理解

I agree.

同意。

Column make當成「讓某人做某事」的意思使用時，有「**勉強（強制）**」的意思。要注意的是，接在受詞後面的動詞必須改回原形（這種用法與have、let一樣）。

She made him do the work.「她讓他做那件工作。」
He will make her buy his lunch.「他差遣她去買他的午餐。」

119

基本中的基本動詞 Top10 [Make] 9/10

　　make的意思原本是「加工某項材料，製成其他物品」，但還有很多其他的意思，而且光是主要用法，就有「製作」「準備」「引起」「讓某人做某事」「做、舉辦」「抵達」「覺得」「到達」「勾搭（女性）」「前進」等意思，若能熟用這個動詞，英文的表現能力就會更多元囉。

視察指令

①「製作；預備、準備」

Could you **make** the documents **ready** for the inspection?

可以幫我準備視察需要的文件嗎？

⇒ make ～ ready
做～的準備

②「讓某事發生」

Don't **make noise** while I'm listening to music.

聽音樂的時候，請不要發出噪音。

⇒ make noise
發出聲音、騷動

③「讓～轉換成某種狀態」

This old song **makes** me feel calm.

這首老歌讓我感覺平靜。

④「讓某人做某事」（使役動詞）

He is trying to **make** me do the job.

他試著讓我做那件工作。

I'm afraid I can't **make** it this time.

很抱歉，這次好像行不通。

⇒ I'm afraid (to say) ～
很抱歉，但是～

Comics Businessman Zombie Tom [19]

First, could you make a reservation at the restaurant, "Domino"?
首先，可以請你預約「多米諾」這家餐廳嗎？

Make a reservation for that hotel, too.
也順便預約那間旅館。

⇒ **make a reservation**
　預約

This isn't a vacation, right?
今天沒休假嗎？

What makes you think that?
是什麼讓妳有這種想法的？

⇒ **Why do you think so?**
　就是「為什麼妳會這麼想？」的意思

Those clothes make you look as if you are on vacation.
你穿成那樣，看起來簡直就像是在休假。

Make 的慣用句

視察的準備

湯姆

老闆

Did you finish making preparations for the inspection?

視察的準備搞定了嗎？

⇒ make preparations for ～
做好～的準備

No, not yet.

還沒。

Can you make the deadline?

趕得上期限吧？

⇒ make the deadline
趕得上期限

I think I can make the 6:00 p.m. train. I can arrive home at seven o'clock.

我趕得上下午6點的電車。7點就可以到家了。

I can't make out what you're saying.

你在講什麼我根本聽不懂。

⇒ make out + what
了解、理解

湯姆報告視察結果

老闆

湯姆

They made a breakthrough by developing something new.

他們透過新開發有了突破性成長。

⇒ **make a breakthrough**
大發現、突破性成長

I am making an effort to reach a general agreement.

我會努力讓多數人達成共識。

⇒ **make an effort (to~)**
努力～

⇒ **general**
大致上、整體的、綜合的

Make sure you do it properly.

我一定會讓你確實執行。

⇒ **make sure**
讓……變得確實、
一定會努力做～

I think Tom made up a story.
我覺得湯姆在捏造事實。

⇒ **make up ～**
捏造（藉口、事實）

What on earth are they developing?
他們到底在開發什麼呢？

⇒ **on earth**
到底（整體來說）

Hear

八卦

hear-heard-heard/hears/hearing

①「聽得見」　②「聽到（謠言、八卦）」

I've **heard** a lot about you.

我聽到你的種種事情。

⇒ **hear about** ～
聽到～的事情

It's been bumpy recently.

最近過得不怎麼順利。

⇒ **bumpy**
很坎坷、命途多舛

I'm glad to **hear** that you became a zombie.

我很高興聽到你成為殭屍。

⇒ **be glad to hear (that)** ～
很開心聽到～

Survival Talk

don't want to hear　不想聽

I don't want to hear your excuses.
我不想聽你的藉口。
→盡可能讓自己站在說這句話的立場。

Have you heard anything about Mr. Ken?

有聽說肯先生什麼消息嗎？

Did you hear what happened to him?

你有聽到他發生什麼事嗎？

This is just between you and me, I heard Mr. Ken has fallen in love.

偷偷告訴你，我聽說肯先生談戀愛了。

⇒ between you and me
偷偷告訴你、這是祕密

Mr. Ken has fallen in love!

肯先生戀愛了！

Huh? I can't hear you well.

蛤？我沒聽清楚。

Yes, I can hear you, but with who?

嗯，我聽到了喇。是跟誰啊？

聽老闆講話

①「聽得見」

Tom, can you hear me?
湯姆，聽得到我的聲音嗎？

Yes, I can hear you.
嗯，聽得到喲。

Do you hear me?
你有認真聽我說嗎？

②「聽到（謠言、八卦）」

I heard that he loves her.
我聽說他愛她。

⇒ hear(that)
　聽說～

Oh, by the way, I haven't heard much about you lately.
話說回來，最近沒聽到你的八卦耶。

Where have you been every day?
你每天都在哪裡啊？

I was here!
我都在這裡啊！

Comics Businessman Zombie Tom [20]

Who is talking about my love life?

是誰在聊我的戀情啊？

I've never heard about that.

我從來沒聽說過那件事耶。

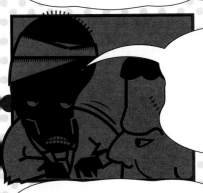

I think Fiona will be delighted to hear that you love her.

要是費歐娜聽到你喜歡她，
肯定會很開心的喲。

I'm looking forward to hearing from you soon.

希望能很快聽到你的回應。

⇒ hear from ～
　　有來自～的聯絡（消息）

Why do I have to answer to you?

為什麼我非得回答你不可？

要不要休個長假？

湯姆

老闆

I heard zombies can take really long vacations.

我聽說殭屍可以休個長假。

If you quit this job, you can take a long vacation. But, I don't want to hear from you after you quit.

辭掉工作，你就可以休長假了啦。
不過辭職後，別再讓我聽到你的消息。

By the way, have you heard anything about the new boss?

話說回來，
你有聽說新老闆什麼事嗎？

Who is the new boss?
新老闆是誰啊？

莎耶很期待殭屍大騷動

莎耶

I couldn't hear the alarm ringing.

我沒聽到警報響起耶。

I heard it was a zombie panic.

我聽說剛剛那是一場殭屍騷動（恐慌）。

I was very surprised to hear that.

我聽到那件事，覺得很驚訝。

I want to hear all about the zombie panic.

我想聽到所有與殭屍騷動有關的事。

Saya is looking forward to hearing about it.

莎耶似乎很期待聽到那些事情。

⇒ look forward to ～
期待～

Leave

出門接待

leave-left-left/leaves/leaving

① 「離去、離開、出發」　② 「忘記拿走」　③ 「留下」
④ 「託付、交辦」　⑤ 「讓～保持原狀」

Are you getting ready to leave?

你準備好要出門了嗎？

Please leave me alone.

請不用管我。

⇒ leave ～ alone
　放著～不管

I'll leave the work up to you.

可是我把這件工作交給你了。

⇒ leave ～ (up) to ...
　把～交給……

Survival Talk

be left behind　被拋下

If you don't try your best, you'll be left behind.

如果你不盡全力，你就會被拋下。

→請把這句話當成是殭屍世界的座右銘。

Can we leave here at six this evening?

下午6點能從這裡出發嗎？

I know how to get there. Leave it to me.

我知道怎麼去那裡，請交給我帶路吧。

Would you mind if I leave early today?

話說，你介意我今天提早下班嗎？

⇒ leave early
提早下班

How can I get there?
我該怎麼去那裡？

I left him at the front gate.

我跟他在大門的地方分開。

搭計程車出去

①「離去、離開、出發」

Is the taxi leaving on schedule?

計程車會如預期出發嗎？

⇒ on schedule
如預期

②「忘記拿走」

I left the important documents at the office.

我把重要的文件忘在公司了。

③「留下」

May I leave a message?

我可以留個話嗎？

④「託付、交辦」

I'll leave everything to you.

之後就都交給你囉。

⑤「讓～保持原狀」

Oh, don't leave the door open.

啊，別讓門一直開著。

Comics Businessman Zombie Tom [21]

Oh my God!

啊，糟糕了！

Leave it at that for today.

今天就先到此為止吧。

⇒ **leave it at that**
　　到此為止、放棄（討論或會議）

Please leave everything as it is.

請就這樣放著，不用多管。

Please leave me out of it.

別把我也捲進去。

⇒ **leave ～ out of ...**
　　把～排除在……之外、拿掉

You should leave it unsaid.

這種事別說出來比較好喲。

133

Leave 的慣用句

雅思的婚前旅行

雅思

飯店服務人員

I'm leaving for a new land tomorrow.

明天我要朝全新的生活出發。

⇒ leave for ～
朝～出發

I think I'll leave with my girlfriend.

我大概會跟她一起去。

Please leave everything to me.

後續所有的事，請都交給我辦。

Where should I leave this baggage?

請問這件行李想放在哪裡呢？

**That's not baggage.
It's my girlfriend.**

這不是行李，是我的女朋友。

134

找到失蹤者了

殭屍研究員

It's been six months since he left home.

他離家出走 6 個月了。

I'll just leave it as it is.

不過，我只能隨它去吧。

We left his name off the list.

我從清單拿掉他的名字。

⇒ leave ～ off
把～排除在……之外、拿掉

I'm feeling left out.

我覺得（自己）被拋棄。

⇒ feel left out
感到被排擠

missing
person

Ahhhhh

He became a zombie.
Take it or leave it.

他變成殭屍了。
要收容他，還是拋棄他呢？

135

Know

湯姆的腳在哪裡？

know-knew-known/knows/knowing

① 「知道、已經知道、了解、理解」　② 「認識、有交情」

Do you know where my leg is?

你知道我的腳在哪裡嗎？

How would I know that?

我怎麼可能會知道。

As far as I know, it was at the dump site.

⇒ **As far as I know**
就我所知

就我所知，好像在垃圾場。

How did you know that?

為什麼妳會知道呢？

I put your leg in the trash.

是我把你的腳丟進垃圾筒的啊。

Do you know what I'm saying?
I didn't know it was your leg.

你懂我說什麼嗎？
我並不知道那是你的腳喲。

You know, my foot is not disposable.

妳應該知道吧，
我的腳可不是可拋式的耶。

⇒ **disposable**
可拋式的、用完即丟的

Survival Talk

nobody knows 誰都不知道

Nobody knows what's going to happen tomorrow or in the next second. 沒有人知道明天或下1秒會發生什麼事。

→不只殭屍的世界如此，想要活下去就得掙扎求生。

打掃到湯姆的腳

① 「知道、已經知道、了解、理解」

Does anyone know who owns this leg?
有誰知道這隻腳是誰的呢？

I know someone who needs it.
我認識需要那隻腳的人喲。

② 「認識、有交情」
I have known him for years.
我認識他很多年了。

⇒ **for years**
　　很多年

> **I'd like to know about Tom's leg.**
> 我想知道湯姆的腳去哪了。

> **I throw it away.**
> 我丟掉囉。

⇒ **throw away ～**
　　丟掉～

Comics Businessman Zombie Tom [22]

You know what?
I made a leg out of tin.
你知道這是什麼嗎？我用錫做了隻腳喲。
I knew you could do it.
我就知道你辦得到。
I never knew you had such a talent.
我不知道你有那項才能。
I don't know how to thank you.
我不知道該怎麼道謝。
But, you know, it's very heavy.
不過，你知道吧，那隻腳很重。

⇒ **You know what?**
你知道這是什麼嗎
（稍微聽一下我要說的）

Know 的慣用句

幫忙肯先生告白

肯先生　　　　　　　　　湯姆

I'd like to know what she feels about me.

我想知道她是怎麼看待我的。

I don't know how to tell my true feelings to Fiona.

我不知道該怎麼向費歐娜表達我的心意。

I know. We have to find an appropriate way.

我懂！我們非想個適當的方法不可。

Can I leave it to you?

我可以交待給你嗎？

I don't know if it is a good idea.

我不知道這是不是個好主意。

I know what.

我有好點子。

140

肯先生好像被甩了

梅杜莎   莎耶

You'll never know what may happen to Mr. Ken.

妳肯定不知道肯先生發生了什麼事。

His sincere personality is known to everybody.

大家都知道他是個老實人。

⇒ **be known to ～**
廣為人知的

As you know, he loves Fiona.

如您所知，他很喜歡費歐娜

⇒ **As you know**
如你所知、如您所知

He knows that he missed a good chance.

他知道自己錯過了機會。

**Oh, really?
I didn't know that.**

咦，真的嗎？
我不知道有這件事。

141

Run

趕不上簡報

run-ran-run/runs/running

《不及物動詞》①「沿著……、跑、流動」 ②「運作」 ③「候選」 ④「上映」
《及物動詞》⑤「移動、讓……跑動」 ⑥「經營」

We ran two kilometers to the station.

我們到車站跑了2公里。

I ran the risk of breaking my leg.

我冒著腳會骨折的危險。　　　　　　　　　　⇒ **run the risk of (-ing)** ～
　　　　　　　　　　　　　　　　　　　　　　　冒著做～的危險。

run into ～　撞見～

I ran into a zombie yesterday. 昨天，我撞見殭屍。
→run into～（可預期的）、run across～（不可預期的）、
　come across～（在行動途中撞見 📖 p.70）

We ran over time when wandering the streets.

在街上跑來跑去，會拖過時間啦。

⇒ run over time
　超過、拖長

Why is there a
coast here?
為什麼這裡是海岸？

We ran our eyes over the map.

我們大致看過這張地圖了。

⇒ run *one's* eyes
　over ~
　大致看過

The National Highway 16 runs along the coast.

國道16號線是沿著海岸走的吧。

Why are there
wild boars here?
為什麼這裡會有山豬？

We ran across a wild boar parent and child.

我們偶然遇見山豬爸爸與小山豬。

⇒ run across ~
　與~不期而遇

⇒ a parent and child
　（一對）親子

We are running late for the presentation.

我們這次的簡報已經遲到了。

⇒ be running late
　已經遲到（通常會用現在進行式）。

143

動詞PAPAGO 〔**Run**〕

奮鬥！殭屍總統山姆

《不及物動詞》①「沿著……、跑、流動」

Sam ran toward his robot.

山姆朝著他的機器人跑過去。

②「運作」

His robot runs on batteries.

他的機器人是靠電池運作的。

⇒ run on ～
靠～（燃料）運作

③「候選」

Sam ran for the presidential election and was elected.

山姆成為總統候選人，而且當選了。

④「上映」

This film is running four times a day.

這部電影一天上映4次。

《及物動詞》⑤「移動、讓……跑動」

Sam ran his robot into the parking area.

山姆讓機器人移動到停車場。

⑤「經營」

Sam is running a movie theater, too.

山姆也經營電影院。

He is always running
films starring himself.

他總是只上映自己當主角的電影。

Comics Businessman Zombie Tom [23]

The wild boars run every four minutes.

山豬每隔4分鐘跑一次。

⇒ **run after** ～
追著～跑

The primitive man is running after the wild boar.

原始人一直追著山豬跑。

I saw the primitive man running away from the wild boar.

我看到原始人從山豬身邊跑開。

⇒ **run away from** ～
從～逃走、離家出走

Run for it!
快逃！

⇒ **run for it**
直線往前逃跑

Ahhhh!

145

錢德無法不進食

錢德

We've run out of meals.

我們吃完食物了。

⇒ run out of ～
用完～、～沒有了

We've run out of time.

我們沒有時間了。

The meal is running late.

太晚用餐了。

⇒ run late
太晚

I ran after my meal, I mean people.

我追著食物跑，也就是追著人類。

This news will be run in tomorrow's newspaper.

這條新聞應該會登上明天的報紙吧。

⇒ be run in the newspaper
登上報紙

山姆與前女朋友不期而遇

山姆

I ran across my ex-girlfriend yesterday.

我昨天碰見前女友了。

⇒ ex-girlfriend
前女友

I ran the risk of speaking to her.

我冒著生命危險跟她搭話。

Our love contract has already run out.

戀人契約已經過期了喲。

⇒ run out
（契約）過期、無效

Sam ran towards the sunset.

山姆朝著夕陽跑過去。

Basic Verb 24
Keep

跟湯姆的朋友喝酒

keep-kept-kept/keeps/keeping

① 「持續」　② 「維持、保存」　③ 「維持某個狀態」
④ 「守護、記錄」　⑤ 「持續做〜」

Sorry to have kept you waiting.

抱歉，讓你久等了。

⇒ keep 〜 -ing
讓〜保持……的狀態

You should keep your promise.

你應該遵守自己的約定喲。

⇒ keep *one's* promise
遵守〜的約定

⇒ keep 〜 in mind
留心〜、記住〜

I'll keep that in mind.

我會留心這件事的。

Survival Talk

keep 〜 in order　讓〜遵守秩序 (社會風俗)

I have to keep the zombies in order.
我必須遵守殭屍的規範。

→ 必須嚴格取締隨便攻擊人類的行為。謹守分際很重要。

Oops, where did I keep my wallet?

咦？錢包收哪裡去？

HA HA HA HA
My wrist broke.
我的手腕斷掉了。

I keep my money in the bank.

我都把錢存在銀行喲。

Are you broke?

沒錢嗎？

⇒ **broke**
沒錢、身無分文

You can keep the change.

找錢就不用了。

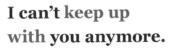

I can't keep up with you anymore.

我再也跟不上你了。

⇒ **keep up with ～**
跟上～

動詞PAPAGO〔Keep〕

基本中的基本動詞 Top10　[Keep]

　　keep的基本用法是「讓事物的狀態或位置保留、維持一段相對較長的時間」。只要了解這個基本用法，就不難理解keep。舉例來說，keep you waiting的意思是「讓你久等了」，此時可解釋成讓「等」這個狀態維持住的意思。keep a dairy「寫日記」可解釋成「長期寫日記」，keep in touch「聯絡」則可解釋成「保持聯絡」。

跟朋友喝酒

①「持續」
I still keep many photos of my school days.
我到現在都還留著許多學生時代的照片。

②「維持、保存」
I'll always keep you in my mind.
不管過了多久，都會記得你。

③「維持某個狀態」
I'll keep in contact with you.
我會跟你聯絡。

⇒ **keep in contact[touch] with**
　　與～取得連繫

④「守護、記錄」
I am keeping a diary.
我一直都有在寫日記。

⑤「持續做～」
We kept drinking until late at night.
我們一直喝到很晚。

⇒ **keep -ing**
　　持續做～

> **Let's keep being good friends.**
> 讓我們繼續當好朋友吧。

> I have no idea who he is.
> 我不知道他是誰？

Column 要注意keep「**讓……保持～的狀態**」這種用法。

Please keep the door open.「請讓門就這樣開著。」
I keep my desk clean.「我會讓桌面保持乾淨。」

Comics Businessman Zombie Tom [24]

Did you keep the beer cool?

可以幫我冰鎮一下啤酒嗎？

Of course it's cold.

啤酒當然是冰的囉。

I'm broke. Please keep it a secret.

我破產了。幫我保守這個祕密。

⇒ keep ～ a secret
保守～祕密

I'll keep it in mind. I'm the same, though.

我會記在心上的。不過我也一樣（沒錢）。

⇒ keep on -ing
持續做～

Can you keep on running?

你還能繼續跑嗎？

I'm okay. I'm keeping in good condition these days.

沒問題，最近（身體的狀況）維持得不錯。

⇒ in good condition
狀態良好

Keep 的慣用句

山姆的健康診療①

山姆

羅伯特

I keep on eating even when I'm not hungry.

我肚子不餓也是繼續吃。

Keep telling yourself not to eat when you are not hungry.

我都一直跟自己說，肚子不餓就不要吃。

⇒ keep on -ing / keep -ing
這兩種都是「持續做〜」的意思，但有「on」的這邊有強調「持續做〜」的意思。

Please keep away from crowds.

請盡量遠離人群。

⇒ keep away from 〜
不要接近〜、避開〜

> I'll keep on trying, starting tomorrow.
> 從明天開始，我會維持下去的。

152

山姆的健康診療②

山姆

You should keep away from eating too much.

你應該避免吃太多。

You should keep the brains out of your reach.

你應該把大腦收在手搆不到的地方。

⇒ keep ～ out of (*one's*) reach
把～收在／放在（某個人）碰不到的位置

Let's keep in touch with each other.

讓我們保持聯絡吧。

Let's keep doing our best and aim to be healthy zombies.

我的目標是盡一切努力，
做個健康的殭屍。

Think

擊退殭屍的社區會議

think-thought-thought/thinks/thinking

①「想、思考」　②「想起」

Just think of our losses.

請想想我們遭受的損失。

⇒ think of ～
思考～的事情

What makes you think that way?

是什麼讓妳這麼想？

⇒ Why do you think that way?
這兩句話的意思相同

We should think again about protecting the zombies.

⇒ think again (about ～)
（對於～）重新思考、再想想

我們應該重新思考保護殭屍這件事吧。

I think she is correct about that point.

就這點來說，我覺得她是對的。

Don't think badly of the zombies, please.

請不要把殭屍想成壞人。

⇒ **think badly of** ～
把～想成不好的事

I've heard it's becoming less safe.

我聽說最近治安變得很差喲。

I think we'll be able to coexist with the zombies!

我覺得我們可以跟殭屍和平共存！

⇒ **coexist with** ～
與～共存

We should think positive when we face a difficulty.

遇到困難，應該保持樂觀的想法。

⇒ **think positive**
正面思考

think so 　 如此覺得

→ 戴口罩的女性靠近後，問你 Do you think I'm pretty?「我漂亮嗎？」
You really **think so**?「你真的如此覺得？」的話，要記得回答 Yes, you
have your own sense of fashion. I **think so**.「沒錯，我覺得你有你自己
的品味」。

動詞PAPAGO 〔**Think**〕

山姆愛上莎曼珊

① 「想、思考」

She looks nice, don't you think?
你不覺得她很漂亮嗎？

I thought she was unmarried.
我以為她還沒結婚。

② 「想起」

I'm trying to think where I met her before.
我好像想起之前曾見過她。

I can't think about anything else.
我沒辦法思考其他的事情。

⇒ think about ～
思考～

Will she go on a date with me?
她會跟我約會嗎？

⇒ go on a date
☞ p.21

You should think it over before you answer that question.
在回答這個問題之前，你應該仔細想想喔。

⇒ think over ～
多想想～

Comics Businessman Zombie Tom [25]

We have to keep the zombies in order.

我們應該要求殭屍守秩序。

When do you think you can finish the job?

你覺得你什麼時候可以結束這件工作呢？

⇒ keep ～ in order
p.148

Do you think you can help us with our work?

你覺得你可以幫我們完成這件工作嗎？

I don't think he is fit for this work.

我不覺得他適合這件工作。

向湯姆道歉的
殭屍糾察隊二人組

秋霞　　　　　　　　　　　　阿玉

Come to think of it, you are a zombie.

現在想起來，你也是殭屍耶。

⇒ come to think of it
想一想

Don't think bad things about us, please.

請別把我們想成壞人。

⇒ think bad things about ～
把～想成不好的事情

I would think again before I accept the offer.

在接受這件事情之前，我會仔細想想。

All I do is think about my hunger.

我能想的只有
肚子空空的這件事。

⇒ All I do is (to) ～
我所要做的是～

莎曼珊是別人老婆

山姆

You are thinking about another woman.

你正在想其他女人吧。

But, I think highly of her work performance.

我很欣賞她的工作態度喲。

⇒ think highly of ～
給予～高評價

Don't think about going out with her.

我勸你打消跟她交往的念頭。

⇒ go out with ～
與～交往、與～來往

You should think over our advice.

你最好仔細想想
我們的忠告喲。

She is married.
她已經結婚了。

Find

被關在門外的湯姆

find-found-found/finds/finding

①「發現、找到」　②「了解」

I can't find my house key.

我找不到家裡的鑰匙。

I found that my wife is out at a meeting.

我發現老婆去參加（社區）會議。

⇒lock out
把～關在外面（不小心或是故意上鎖）

I locked myself out.

我被關在門外。

I was not able to find the money.

我沒辦法找到錢。

I found there is nothing in this house.

我發現這個家裡什麼都沒有。

What are you doing in my house?
你在我家做什麼？

Who are you?

你是誰？

It's okay. I'm trying to find a new house.

沒問題，我會再找一個新家。

湯姆尋獲錢包了

①「發現、找到」

I found a wallet on my way home.
我在回家途中尋獲一個錢包了。

I can't find the time to go to the police station.
我沒有時間去派出所。

②「了解」

I found the way to the police station.
我知道怎麼去派出所。

I found out I was wrong.
我知道自己的錯誤。

⇒ find out (that)
　了解、知道、發現～（那件事情）

I found out the truth.
I found a karaoke box
there.
我發現事實了。那裡有間卡拉OK。

Survival Talk

you can find it　你能找到那個

If you look carefully, you can find it.
仔細觀察，就能發現它。
→要發現剛成為殭屍的人，需要有極佳的觀察力。

Comics Businessman Zombie Tom [26]

Tell me what you are doing.

請告訴我，你在做什麼。

I found myself in bed at your house.

回過神來才發現，我已經在你家床上。

⇒ found *oneself* ＋場所
發現自己在意料之外的場所、
回過神才發現自己在莫名的地方

I found this house is very easy to break into.

我發現這個家很容易闖入耶。

Look, I found an ugly tie.

你看，我還找到一條很醜的領帶喲。

⇒ ugly
醜

He seems to try to find fault with my house.

他好像正在挑我家的毛病。

⇒ find fault with ～
挑～的毛病、對～找碴、批評～

Find 的慣用句

湯姆正在找派出所

湯姆   小偷

Excuse me. I'm trying to find the police station.

不好意思，我正在找派出所。

⇒ **try to find ～**
打算找～

You'll find it next to the bakery at the intersection.

你會在十字路口的麵包店旁邊找到喲。

⇒ **next to ～**
在～的旁邊

However, I don't think I can find my way back home.

可是，我好像找不到回家的路。

⇒ ***one's* way back home**
回某個人的家

I can go with you. I know where to find your house.

我跟你一起去吧。
我知道在哪裡可以找到你家。

⇒ **where to find ～**
在哪裡可以找到～

被逮捕的小偷

湯姆

警察

I didn't have any trouble finding my way back home.

順利找到回家的路了。

⇒ **have trouble -ing**
做～的時候遇到麻煩（問題）

Thank you for finding Tom.

感謝你幫我找到湯姆。

⇒ **thank you for -ing**
感謝你幫我做～

After taking a close look, I found out he was a thief.

仔細一看之後，才發現他是小偷。

⇒ **take a close look**
仔細一看

I will find out what he was doing.

我會調查他
幹了哪些好事。

⇒ **find out + what** 子句
調查、找出～

165

Basic Verb 27
Call

街上出現殭屍騷動

call-called-called/calls/calling

① 「打電話」　② 「呼叫、稱呼」　③ 「簡單的拜訪、順路」　④ 「召集」

The zombie *break* dance was called off because of rain.

殭屍霹靂舞因為下雨而被迫中止了。

⇒ **call off**
中止

There are a great number of zombies walking around in the city.

街上有很多殭屍在徘徊。

⇒ **walk around**
徘徊

It's okay, a hero will call on us.

沒問題，英雄會來找（解決問題）我們啦。

⇒ **call on ～**
拜訪某人、順路去某人的地方

Did you call out for me?

是妳大聲呼叫我的嗎？

⇒ **call out for ~**
大聲呼叫~

I called for help again and again.

我已經多次尋求幫助了。

⇒ **call for ~**
（強烈）尋求、
訴求~

I admire the way you handle zombies.

我很欣賞妳處置殭屍的方法耶。

⇒ **admire ~**
欣賞、佩服~

Handle your own
problems by yourself.
自己的問題得自己解決。

Anyway, could you call the police for me?

總之，你可以幫我叫警察嗎？

You call them by yourself.

自己打電話吧。

英雄終於來了

①「打電話」
Please call the police at once.
請立刻打電話給警察。

②「呼叫、稱呼」
My name is Jones. Please call me J.
我的名字叫瓊斯,請叫我J就好。

③「簡單的拜訪、順路」
I just called on you at your city.
我去你住的地方,簡單的拜訪你一下。

④「召集」
I am being called by a party of heroes.
同為英雄的夥伴叫我去參加他們的派對。

Goodbye.

Please call me again.
記得再呼叫我喲。

Survival Talk

Let's call it quits.　就此結束吧!
→為了精采的最後一集,要記住這句話喔。

Comics Businessman Zombie Tom [27]

What do you call that technique in Chinese?

這一招的中文叫什麼？

I'll call up that information on the internet.

我在網路上查查看。

⇒ call up ～
　調出、調查（資訊）

You have a black belt in judo, right?

你是柔道黑帶嗎？

I'll call in sick for you. Please fight as much as you want.

我會在妳躺下休息的時候幫妳打電話。
請盡情戰鬥吧。

⇒ call in sick
　因病休息時，打電話告知。

Call 的慣用句

順道去殭屍義大利餐廳的錢德先生

錢德

Let's call in at John's shop after work.

工作結束後,順道去約翰的店吧。

⇒ call in at ～
順道去某個地點、中途停車

If your name is called, please enter the room.

叫到您的名字,就請進來房間。

What's it called? I've never had that before.

那道菜叫什麼名字呢?我沒吃過那道菜。

It's called intestinal pasta.

這道菜叫腸子義大利麵。

It's not polite to slurp when you eat intestinal pasta.
吃腸子義大利麵的時候,最好不要發出吸麵的聲音,不然會很失禮。

⇒ slurp
喝東西、吸麵的時候發出聲音

搭訕莎耶的
英雄 J

莎耶

J

Let's call it a day and have a beer.

今天就到此為止吧，我們去喝杯啤酒。

⇒ **call it a day**
（今天的工作）到此為止、結束、收工；與「to stop working for the day」是相同意思。

Please call me J. So, can I call you S?

叫我 J 就好，所以我能叫妳 S 嗎？

I don't want to be called that.

我不想被這樣叫。

Don't hesitate to call me.

不用客氣，儘管打電話給我。

I'm calling your bluff.

我已經看透你在虛張聲勢。

⇒ **bluff**　　　⇒ **call *one's* bluff**
虛張聲勢、吹牛　　看穿某人虛張聲勢

I'll call you in a million years.
要我打電話，等一百萬年吧。

Speak

「說話的動詞」
Tell、Say、Talk、**Speak**（說話）

殭屍工會

speak-spoke-spoken/speaks/speaking

①「說話」　②「演說、陳述」

We will make an announcement about forming the zombie union.

我們在此發表，組成殭屍工會。

Can you speak more slowly, please?

可以說得慢一點嗎？

Don't speak with your mouth full, please.

請不要在嘴巴塞滿東西的時候說話。

Survival Talk

speak clearly　說得清楚

→殭屍很常像是含著滷蛋說話，所以這也是分辨他們的方法之一。
不過也有報告指出The more the zombies spoke, the more they improved.，意思是他們越常說話，話會說得越好。所以請大家務必多多注意喔。

Why are you forming it?

為什麼會組成（工會）呢？

Please speak only about the truth.

請告訴我們實情。

You speak!

你說啦！

Why me?

為什麼是我？

Frankly speaking, you are silly.

坦白說，你很蠢耶。

⇒ **frankly speaking**
坦白地說

They are no longer speaking.

他們再也不說半句話。

⇒ **no longer**
再也不～

記者打電話來採訪

①「說話」

This is Mr. Woodward speaking.
你好,我叫伍華德。

May I speak to the union president, Mr. Robert?
電話可以轉給工會會長羅伯特先生嗎?。

⇒ **may I speak to ～**
可以把電話轉給～

Speaking.
我就是。

Let me hear you speak your mind.
我想聽聽您真實的想法。

⇒ **speak *one's* mind**
坦率的說出想法

②「演說、陳述」

I asked one question, and he spoke on and on for an hour.
我只問一個問題,結果他滔滔不絕演講了一個小時。

⇒ **on and on**
滔滔不絕

They have no purpose to speak of.
他們沒有什麼重點可說的。

⇒ **no ～ to speak of**
沒什麼可說的～

say/ speak/ talk/ tell的概念 ☞ p.48

174

Comics Businessman Zombie Tom [28]

We don't speak the same language.

我們沒辦法跟彼此溝通。

⇒ **speak the same language**
超過2人以上的想法相同、互相了解

Tom always speaks against the union principles.

湯姆總是反對工會的方針。

⇒ **speak against ～**
發表反對～的言論
cf. speak in favor of ～
發表贊成～的言論

Robert is, so to speak, a puppet.

要我說的話，羅伯特就像是傀儡吧。

⇒ **so to speak**
要我說的話

Don't speak ill of me.

別說我壞話。

⇒ **speak ill of ～**
別說～的壞話

Whew.

哎呀呀。

羅伯特的聲音很小

Could you speak up a little?

說話的聲音可以再大一點嗎？

⇒ speak up
提高音量說話

Robert speaks like a little girl.

羅伯特說話總像個小女孩。

⇒ speak like ～
像～般說話

I think it is better to speak in a more masculine way.

我覺得應該說得像男子漢會更好。

⇒ speak in a ～ way
說得像～的樣子

⇒ masculine
有男子氣概

Speaking of Robert, I agree with your opinion, and everyone would also agree with you.

說到羅伯特，我是贊成你的意見，
大家也贊成你吧。

⇒ speak of ～
說到～

I don't want to speak with anyone.

我不想跟任何人說話。

⇒ speak with ～
跟～說話

湯姆的英語很糟

湯姆

羅伯特

Please feel free to speak out against our idea.

請不客氣地大聲反對我們的意見。

⇒ **speak out against**
公開反對、大聲疾呼地反對

You speak German very well, but can you speak to me in English?

你的德語說得很好，那你可以跟我說英語嗎？

⇒ **speak to ～**
與～搭話

Ha Ha Ha! Now, you're speaking my language.

哈哈哈！現在總算能了解彼此了。

⇒ **speak *one's* language**
與～的想法相同、了解彼此

Hold

整個社區洋溢幸福

hold-held-held/holds/holding

① 「持有、擁抱、握住、抓住」　② 「舉辦、召開」
③ 「就職、就任、擁有記錄、稱號」　④ 「保有、保持」
⑤ 「具有意見（信念、評價）、認為」　⑥ 「套入、套用」

The couples are holding hands and walking.

情侶牽著手走路。

The world is at peace.
世界一片祥和。

A mother is holding her baby on her lap.

母親把小寶寶抱在腿上。

Survival Talk

hold back　抑制、制止

The government tries to hold back the zombies, but it faces difficult problems.

政府雖然極力制止殭屍，卻遇上了難題。

→ 先確認防災用品吧。

I broke my leg again.
我的腳又折斷了。

He is holding a leg in his hand.

他把斷腳拿在手上。

The zombie is being held down by a woman.

殭屍被女性壓在地上。

⇒ hold down ~
壓制~

My waitress is being held up.

女服務生的動作很慢。

Still, I believe the world is at peace.
即使如此，我還是相信
世界一片祥和。

Hold them up!

舉手投降！

⇒ still
即使如此，
還是……、仍然

⇒ hold up
很慢、支撐、撐住、命令停止、
舉高（雙手或物品）、套用（想
法或證據）

179

大衛是個花心蘿蔔

① 「持有、擁抱、握住、抓住」
Kate holds a knife.
凱特握著一把小刀。

② 「舉辦、召開」
I will hold a goodbye party for David.
我打算替大衛舉辦餞別會。

③ 「就職、就任、擁有記錄、稱號」
I've held a position as his girlfriend for three years.
我這3年都在他的身邊，擁有戀人的地位。

④ 「保有、保持」
Hold your horses, Kate.
凱特，保持冷靜，不要慌。

⇒ Hold your horses.
不要慌。

⑤ 「具有意見 (信念、評價)、認為」
I hold that David is responsible.
我認為大衛有責任。

⑥ 「套入、套用」
That rule does not hold up in this case.
那項規則不適用於這個情況。

Because I am a zombie.
因為我是個殭屍。

Comics Businessman Zombie Tom [29]

There are many zombies outside!
外面有好多殭屍啊！

Hold on three minutes, please.
請等待3分鐘。

⇒ **hold on**
繼續、保持、不掛斷

I don't have time to hold.
我沒有那麼多時間可以等。

Hold the line, please.
請不要掛斷電話。

⇒ **hold (the line)**
不掛斷電話地等著

Help me!
救命啊！

Hold your tongue.
請保持沉默。

⇒ **hold *one's* tongue**
保持沉默（tongue是「舌頭」的意思）

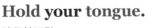

Hold 的慣用句

吃飯皇帝大

金彬

J

J holds an instant noodle cup.

J 拿著泡麵的杯子。

Hold on here. I'll be back soon.

請在這裡等一下,我很快就回來。

Please hold on tight to the rail.

請牢牢抓住欄杆。

⇒ hold on tight to ～
牢牢抓住～

It's dangerous, hold that pose.

很危險,請保持靜止,不要亂動。

Hold on a moment, please.
請稍等一下。

⇒ hold that pose
（保持現在的姿勢）
請不要動（這句話常
用於拍照時）

不能把大家都變成石頭

老闆

I hold you responsible for it.

我認為你得負起那個責任。

⇒ hold ～ responsible for …
對～有……的責任

However, I hold a good opinion of you.

話說回來，我對妳有很不錯的評價喲。

We were held up at work.

工作耽誤了。

I was going to hold a meeting this evening.

我原本打算今晚開會的。

⇒ be going to ～
打算做～

You turned everyone to stone.

妳把所有人變成石像了。

Bring

讓殭屍交流的家庭聚會

bring-brought-brought/brings/bringing

①「帶來（自己的位置）」　②「拿到（對方的位置）」
③「帶去、帶來」　④「造成、到達」

Please bring along your friend. ⇒ bring along
帶來

請帶朋友一起來。

I'll bring my wife to tonight's party.

我會帶老婆來今晚的派對。

I will bring my girlfriend.

我會帶女朋友來喲。

 Survival Talk

Thank you for bringing me into the world.

感謝妳帶我來到這個世上。

→成為殭屍之後，先如此感謝母親，再決定接下來怎麼辦。

Are you bringing your girlfriend Fiona?

你要帶來的女朋友是費歐娜嗎？

No, I'm not, because she is well brought up.

不是，我不會帶她來，因為她的教養良好。

⇒ well brought up
教養良好

Yeah, yeah. I'm sure this party won't be nice.
好吧，我相信這場派對不會太高雅。

I'll bring delicious human brain pickles to the party.

我會帶好吃的人腦醬菜來派對喲。

I want to go, too! Could you bring the car to the front gate?

我也想去！請把車子開來大門這兒。

You are not invited.

沒有人邀請你。

185

動詞PAPAGO 〔Bring〕

準備派對的食材

①「帶來（自己的位置）」
Could you bring me a normal meal, too?
能帶來一些平常的料理嗎？

②「拿到（對方的位置）」
I'll bring it to you by five.
5點之前，我會帶去你那裡。

③「帶去、帶來」
Would you like me to bring some people you can eat as well?
您要我帶去一些可以吃的人類嗎？

④「造成、到達」
That won't be necessary.
We should make friends with people.
This is the conclusion we were brought to.
沒那必要，我的朋友都是人類。
這是我們做出的結論。

⇒ bring ～ to a conclusion
　　將～導向結論

| take | 拿到某個位置（其他的地方）、帶去 ☞p.22 |
| bring | 拿來（去）話題裡的位置、帶來（去） ☞p.184 |

Comics Businessman Zombie Tom [30]

Bring your palms up horizontally and walk unsteadily.

請將掌心水平往上舉，搖搖晃晃地走。

⇒ bring up
往上舉

I acted like a zombie.

我假裝是個殭屍。

Shall I bring a hamburger?

我帶一個漢堡好嗎？

Don't worry. I can't bring myself to eat it.

不用擔心，我怎麼樣也不會想吃那個啦。

⇒ can't bring *oneself* to ～
無論如何也不會想做～

Oh, that's intestinal pasta.

啊，是大腸義大利麵喲。

What brought me here today?

今天我是為了什麼來這裡的啊？

⇒ What brought ～ here?
不知為何，～來到這裡

187

不請自來的老闆

湯姆

老闆

A one-hour drive brought me to Tom's house.

我開了 1 小時的車，總算抵達湯姆的家。

What brought you here?

是什麼風把你吹來這裡？

Well, don't forget to bring back my book.

呃，我的書別忘了還我。

Hey, Tom. Bring him here right away.

喂，湯姆，立刻把他帶進來。

⇒ right away
立刻

Good to see you, Samantha.
很高興見到妳，莎曼珊。

派對結束了

湯姆

The party brought me a lot of trouble.

這個派對為我帶來許多麻煩。
⇒ bring ～ trouble
對～造成麻煩、帶來問題

I'm really tired. Could you bring me a glass of water?

好累啊，能幫我拿杯水來嗎？

OK! By the way, did you know that Mr. Sam brought out a new movie?

嗯。話說回來，妳知道山姆先生發表新電影了嗎？
⇒ bring out
出版、發售

That movie brought back memories of happy days for me.

⇒ bring back ～
帶回～、使回想起來

那部電影讓我想起快樂的回憶。

Every day brings happiness to zombies. Why don't you become one, too?

每一天，殭屍都過得很幸福。妳要不要也成為其中一員呢？

189

【後記】

英師路

Thank you for coming to our party.
感謝你來到我們的派對。

Does this book help people improve their English?
這本書有幫大家提升英語能力嗎？

You are exactly right.
說的一點都沒錯。

This method is sure to work well.
這種方法一定能讓你學得更好。

It won't take long.
也不會花太多時間嘍。

You can take it as a joke.

你可以把它當成笑話聽聽就好。

I take back his words.

我撤銷他的發言。

Why did you publish this book?

為什麼要出版這本書呢？

The author is not here now.

作者目前不在這裡啦。

I won't go into this in detail.

關於這個問題，我不打算詳細說明。

It goes without saying that I'm a zombie.

不說也知道，我是殭屍。

I get hungry all the time.

我肚子總是很餓。

I've got a bad feeling about this.

對此，我有不好的預感。

Please leave everything to us.

請把一切都交給我們吧。

國家圖書館出版品預行編目資料

屍速英語——活用30個學過的基本動詞，職場英語嚇嚇叫！／KAWASEMI
Co., Ltd.、交學社 著；許郁文 譯.
-- 初版. -- 臺北市：如何，2020.08
192面；12.8×18.6公分. --（Happy Languages；163）
ISBN 978-986-136-554-1（平裝）

1.英語 2.讀本

805.18   109008295

Eurasian Publishing Group
圓神出版事業機構
用心閱你對話·細野無限寬廣

如何出版社
Solutions Publishing

www.booklife.com.tw   reader@mail.eurasian.com.tw

Happy Languages 163

屍速英語——活用30個學過的基本動詞，職場英語嚇嚇叫！

作　　者／KAWASEMI Co., Ltd.、交學社
譯　　者／許郁文
發 行 人／簡志忠
出 版 者／如何出版社有限公司
地　　址／台北市南京東路四段50號6樓之1
電　　話／（02）2579-6600·2579-8800·2570-3939
傳　　真／（02）2579-0338·2577-3220·2570-3636
總 編 輯／陳秋月
主　　編／柳怡如
責任編輯／張雅慧
校　　對／張雅慧·柳怡如
美術編輯／金益健
行銷企畫／詹怡慧·曾宜婷
印務統籌／劉鳳剛·高榮祥
監　　印／高榮祥
排　　版／陳采淇
經 銷 商／叩應股份有限公司
郵撥帳號／18707239
法律顧問／圓神出版事業機構法律顧問　蕭雄淋律師
印　　刷／祥峰印刷廠
2020年8月　初版

No way!

I want to eat your pancreas.

Original Japanese title: SALARYMAN ZOMBIE TOM TO MANABU ZOMBIE BUSINESS EIKAIWA
copyright © 2018 Kawasemi, Co., Ltd.
Original Japanese edition published by FUSOSHA publishing Inc.
Traditional Chinese translation right arranged with FUSOSHA Publishing Inc.
through The English Agency (Japan) Ltd. and AMANN CO., LTD., Taipei
Traditional Chinese translation copyright © 2020 by SOLUTIONS PUBLISHING,
an imprint of EURASIAN PUBLISHING GROUP

定價 240 元   ISBN 978-986-136-554-1   版權所有·翻印必究